A MCKENZIE RIDGE NOVELLA

IN JULY

STEPHANIE ST. KLAIRE

CHRISTMAS IN JULY

A MCKENZIE RIDGE NOVELLA

STEPHANIE ST. KLAIRE

COPYRIGHT © 2019
Stephanie St. Klaire
Christmas in July
A McKenzie Ridge Novella

This book is a work of fiction. Names, characters, places, and incidents are either products of the author's imagination or are used fictitiously. Any resemblance to actual events or locales or persons, living or dead, or other status is entirely coincidental.

All rights reserved, including the right to reproduce this book or portions thereof in any form whatsoever known, not known or hereafter invented, or stored in any storage or retrieval system, is forbidden and punishable by the fullest extent of the law without written permission of the author.

EDITOR: Jenny Simms
COVER ARTIST: The SSK Group
FORMATTING: The SSK Group

BOOKS BY STEPHANIE ST. KLAIRE

McKenzie Ridge Series

Rescued

Hidden

Forgotten

Fearless

Redemption

McKenzie Ridge Novellas

Christmas in July

Brother's Keeper Series

Declan (pt 1)

Declan (pt 2)

Liam

Luke

Dace

Wylie

Love, Cass (a series companion novel)

The Keeper's Series

Close Encounter (pt 1)

Close Encounter (pt 2)

Deadly Pursuit

Fatal Diversion

Royal Reckoning

Daddy Diaries

Volume 1

Faux-Mance Novels

Liar

Rumor Has It

Sneaking Around

Bed Buddies

ACKNOWLEDGMENTS

To all who have loved McKenzie and wanted more…
I heard you…
This one is for you!

Merry Christmas…in July!

1

"Cheese and rice." Fifi Gallagher coughed as she stepped out of her car and into a cloud of dust she'd kicked up from driving faster than necessary. "Guess they still haven't discovered pavement out here in the sticks."

She wheezed again. "I think this is what hell is like. Too quiet, no people, and I actually miss the smog."

As the dust began to settle, so did the edgy mood provoked by fifteen hours in a car. A sight Fifi hadn't been witness to in nearly two decades had her attention as she scanned her late grandmother's property. When she was finally able to take a deep, cleansing breath of fresh mountain air, she closed her eyes and let the frustration go as she remembered the reason she was here.

"Wow. I forgot how beautiful it is here. No pavement suddenly makes sense," she said to herself.

She leaned back into the car, reached for her smartphone left in the center console, and made a note to herself.

Scout location: McKenzie Ridge.

"I can't believe nobody has filmed here," Fifi whispered as she slid the device into her back pocket.

"You've got to see this, Dallas," she spoke over her shoulder, closing the front door and switching to the back seat. "You ready to get out of your car seat, buddy?"

A loud snort and a hot, breathy breeze up the back of her shirt startled her. Jumping, she hit her head on the inside roof of the car. When a gentle nudge to her ass and grunt followed, she reached for the closest weapon and lunged back out of the car with a primal grunt of her own.

"Who the hell do you…?" She paused, eyes wide, and let out a bloodcurdling scream.

Fifi Gallagher was fresh out of LA and five minutes in small-town USA only to find herself face-to-face with the most hideous creature she'd met to date. No amount of self-defense or Krav Maga training had prepared her for the one predator she'd never expected a run-in with. Her stun gun didn't stand a chance given his size, nor did the gallons of Mace she packed with her daily. No, she was about to meet her maker at the hands of a short ton killer…

Fifi was standing toe to toe with a *freakin'* buffalo.

When the beast licked its lips with a hungry grumble, and dark, beady eyes fixed on Fifi, she fell into the car, yanked the door closed behind her, and locked it for good measure. Who knew what buffalo were capable of?

"It's okay, Dallas," she said over her shoulder. "Mommy won't let it hurt you!"

With the weapon still in her hand — a black stiletto — she tossed it at the buffalo with all her might. The only problem was the window was rolled up, and the blunt force trauma Fifi was trying to inflict on her would-be attacker bounced right back in her face. *Literally.*

"Fuck!" she yelled, slapping a hand over her now wounded brow.

The animal wasn't standing down. Not even a little. With

one heavy step forward, its head was pressed against the rear window, the air from its nostrils fogging the glass. Well, until a large pink tongue began to *lick* the window.

"Hell no. I had to wait a year for this car to come in!" Fifi wedged herself between the two front seats and laid on the horn in hopes to startle it away. "Get out of here! Go! I'm calling the police…er, animal control!"

"Oh! My phone. I have a phone. Get it together and call for help, Fifi," she said to herself.

Still tightly wedged between the front seats, she finally pulled away from the horn and reached for her back pocket instead.

"Got it," she said, dialing 9-1-1.

When the other line didn't ring, she held out her phone. "What? No bars and out of service? This can't be happening. It's the mountains, not outer space, for fuck's sake. Surely they have a tower nearby."

She held her phone up, turning from left to right, as if the cell signal she desired was mere inches on either side of her. When she saw the buffalo run off in front of the car, she slouched in relief. It was leaving. She and Dallas were safe.

An unexpected tap on the rear window had Fifi jumping and hitting her head on the interior roof again. When she reached up to cradle the back of her head, her carefully balanced weight teetered forward, and she took a face plant to the dash with a solid thud.

"Are you all right?" the man hollered through the glass, knocking more vigorously. "Ma'am? Ma'am…are you okay?"

Pulling herself from the narrow confines between the two front seats, she plopped herself into the back seat and rubbed her forehead. When she looked to her left and saw the man standing there with his eyes still on her, she screamed again.

"Get away from me!" Her hands shuffled around on the floor until she found her previous weapon. "I've...I've... called the police, and I won't hesitate to use this!"

The man straightened, amused eyebrows raised. "You won't hesitate to throw that shoe at the window again? I'm afraid that only hurts you, given what happened a minute ago. And the only place you can get a cell signal on this property is out by the barn."

"Excuse me? How would you know that?" Fifi questioned, his latex-gloved hands catching her attention. "I didn't drive all the way from LA to deal with a squatter. Get off my gram's property, or do you want to wait it out and test your cell signal theory and see if the cops show up?"

If she'd learned anything from living and working in Hollywood with the best-paid liars — *actors* — it was how to sell a convincing fib of her own.

"Gram?" the man questioned.

"Yes!" Fifi said with confidence, spinning another tale. "She's inside right now, calling the sheriff or whatever you all have out here. So, squatter, serial killer, whatever you are, it's jail for you unless you leave now...like, *run* and don't come back, like...ever."

"LA?" The man stepped back as if to get a better view of her. "Fiona? Fiona Gallagher?"

A sharp gasp escaped her. "How do you know my name?"

The man rubbed his hands over his face, the amusement replaced with something that looked like sorrow. "I...uh, know a lot about you."

"You're *stalking* me?" she questioned, then squinted her eyes. "I suppose a serial killer would stalk his prey."

"A what?" he replied. "Serial...no, I'm not a serial killer. Why would a serial killer be all the way out here? That doesn't even make sense."

"Or does it! Maybe you're just saying that to throw me off. Maybe you really are a killer, been following me for days, weeks maybe… Given the rumpled shirt and day-old scruff, I'd say you've been on the road as long as I have. All the way from LA!"

"I think you've been in Hollywood a little too long." He chuckled.

"Still trying to throw me off, huh?" she fired back. "I'm not falling for your…shenanigans. I watch plenty of crime shows, *true crime* shows. I know how your type operates. You try to win me over with that silver fox charm and dimple, get me to trust you with those friendly baby blues…well, I *don't* trust you and will see to it you get life in the slammer. I *know* people."

"You know people? Like what, real lawyers or just people who play them in movies?" He chuckled again, amused by her behavior. "And I assume silver fox is a compliment because being called a serial killer…I have to say, it stings a little."

"In any other case, yes. Right now? No. I just call them as I see them. People don't wander in the desolate areas of small mountain towns with rubber gloves unless they're up to something and trying to avoid leaving fingerprints and, like… DNA, or whatever. And the only way you'd know my name is by googling me," Fifi confirmed.

"No. Dee talked about you all the time." The man smiled. "You were her favorite topic of conversation, actually. That's how I figured out who you were. I feel like I know you. Man, I should have recognized you from the pictures, but I guess I didn't think—"

"She did? I mean…of course she did. We were tight, super tight, so why wouldn't she? Now, tell me who *you* are before…the sheriff gets here. And don't give me one of those aliases you guys try to pass off."

"I live here," the man said. "I knew your grandmother…*very* well."

Fifi's jaw dropped. "You live here? Gram never mentioned… Oh, no. OH, NO! Aren't you a little…*young* for her?"

The man waved his hands in front of him, his shocked expression matching hers. "She was like a mother to me."

"Eww, that makes it worse." Fifi grasped her chest and swallowed hard, trying to hold down the gas station chili dog she knew she'd regret.

"No, no, I live here." He waved his hands around as his body twisted, indicating the property around him. "In the carriage house out back. Not with…not in that way…"

Fifi's shoulders slacked as relief settled in. "Oh, good. I was worried. I mean, you're…so…"

The man cocked one hip and crossed his arms, waiting for what felt like a looming insult. "I'm so what? Besides a charming silver fox with an endearing dimple and day-old scruff. Please, don't stop now, *Hollywood*."

"Hollywood?" She snorted. "Seriously? I was going to say someone so *juvenile*. And it's Fifi. Not *Fiona*. Not *Hollywood*."

"Wow, you're more *Hollywood* than Dee let on," he said under his breath.

"Excuse me?" she chided.

"Oh…uh, I said my name is Bain." He raised his voice, holding up his gloved hands. "*Dr.* Jensen Bain. Surely it's getting hot in there for you two. Why don't you come out?"

Fifi looked him up and down once more, considering her options. Despite being startled by the man initially, he really did seem friendly, and if he was a doctor, the gloves made sense — *or did they?*

"What's a doctor doing out here, in the middle of nowhere, with gloves on…outside?" she asked, still unsure about this Bain guy. "Hold them up again and show me both sides. For all I know, I interrupted your latest conquest."

Dr. Jensen Bain tossed his head back and let out a deep roar of laughter. "My last *patient* is here. Out in the barn."

Fifi's eyes grew wide as she held the stiletto high.

"No…not like *that*. I'm a vet. All my patients come through the barn," he said. "Well…what used to be the barn. It's had a bit of an upgrade. It's where I run my practice. When I'm not making rounds with home visits for the larger patients, I see and treat them here. Dee and I had an agreement. I rent the property and space from her, and she gets free pet care."

"My grandmother doesn't have a pet," Fifi rebutted.

"Exactly, which is why I had Sunday dinner with her instead and helped with the upkeep. It was the least I could do since she didn't charge me nearly enough for this place." He smiled, appreciating the memory of his late friend. "She was a good woman."

Fifi finally climbed out of the car. "I'll have you know that I'm legally obligated to inform you that I am a highly trained martial artist and quite literally a lethal weapon. If you lay a hand on me, I will defend myself by any and all means necessary, even if it ends in your…demise. I'll have you down and out long before that sheriff gets here."

When the man stalled, he dragged his hands over his face once again, "Right, the phone call inside. Look, I…uh, hate to be the one to tell you, but…your gram passed. About a month or so ago. I take it this is a surprise visit? She didn't mention she was expecting you. You know, before she—"

Confusion and exhaustion took over, leaving Fifi with a lacking filter. "Of course I know she passed. Why wouldn't I? I'm her only relative — *close* relative, remember? One she never mentioned having a…tenant to."

Her tears threatened, but Fifi kept them at bay while she figured out who this serial killer squatter was and how to get rid of him. If he was telling the truth, why would her grandmother have kept him a secret? Maybe they weren't as close as she'd thought.

"You said she was inside…calling the police." He looked over his shoulder at the house. "Did you see someone in the window or something?"

With a dramatic eye roll, she fired back, "No. I didn't see my gram or anyone else in the window. I was trying to scare you away."

Bain grinned. "Well, then, we're finally getting somewhere. And I truly am sorry for your loss. I meant what I said about Dee. She was a good woman, respected by everyone who knew her. She'll be missed. I just started the grill. I can throw something on if you're hungry. It's not cheese and rice, but—"

"Cheese and rice?" She snickered. "That sounds…awful."

"Oh? You said cheese and rice when you got out of the car…the first time, so I thought you were hungry."

"Oh! That? No…I was frustrated. I always say that instead of…you know"—Fifi pointed to the heavens—"the J.C. word."

"JC?"

"You know…the big guy upstairs." Fifi pointed toward the sky, more urgent. "Rhymes with cheese and rice…"

"Oh, you mean Jesus Christ." He snorted. "I had no idea you were religious."

"Pfft. I'm not," she chortled. "I just don't like to borrow trouble."

"You're kidding, right?"

Fifi offered Bain a side-eye glance. "No. Not at all."

"But you said plenty of other…" Bain shook his head. "Never mind."

"Oh no!" Fifi shouted as she turned the doc in the direction she was looking and stood behind him. "It's coming back!"

Bain laughed. "Oh, Ben? He's a big ole teddy bear."

"Yeah, last I heard, bears shredded humans and tore them apart, limb by limb."

"They sure do," Bain said as Fifi jumped back in her car. "Back in the car? Seriously?"

The buffalo stood at Bain's side, nudging him until the good doc scratched the animal's head.

"You can come out of there. He isn't going to hurt you. Gentle Ben is just a baby."

"A baby? At that size? His poor mother." Fifi snorted. "He's a little intimidating."

"Just come on out, and you'll see. He hasn't hurt me one bit. He really is gentle. C'mon and meet him. As soon as he meets you, he'll probably take off. He's just curious and wants to know who you are. I think he took Dee's passing the hardest. The two were pals from the first day I brought him here."

Odd, Fifi thought. Why wouldn't her gram mention she lived with a buffalo…as a *pet*? Or the doctor, or the clinic he seemed to run out of here? They were close and talked about everything. *Or so she'd thought.*

Fifi climbed back out of the car. "Well, just because my gram liked him doesn't mean I will."

The buffalo snorted and took a step closer to Fifi, causing her to take a step back.

Bain gently reached for Fifi's hand and gave her a nod as if asking her to trust him. Interestingly enough, she did. He lifted her hand out in front of her, and Ben stepped forward, softly butting his head against it.

"See, he likes you," Bain said. "Kind as can be."

"Well, I suppose it could be worse." She smiled, stroking the length of his face. "But I don't want him around here like this. It won't be good for prospective buyers."

"Buyers?" Bain questioned.

"Yes. That's why I'm here. Say goodbye to my gram and get the place ready to sell. I have no use for it."

"But the animals. There are plenty more than just Ben on the property," Bain said. "Dee loved having them here. Where will they all go?"

"They live here?"

"Some. Most are patients, but some can't be released back into the wild, displaced, or adopted for various reasons."

"Wild animals? Displaced and unadoptable sounds like troubled." Fifi shrugged.

"Troubled?" Bain questioned, irritation setting in. "They're animals, not thugs. They have a home here. The alternative for them is to be euthanized."

"Ooh. That sounds…tragic…and permanent."

"Gee, ya think? Hey, the blanket is moving in there. Do you want to get him or her out?"

"Dallas!" Fifi shouted, diving back into the car. She pulled the blanket off the car seat and began to talk in a small, baby-like voice. "Oh, you poor baby. Mommy didn't mean to leave you in there so long. It was getting warm, huh?"

When Fifi finally backed out of the car and turned to face Bain, his jaw dropped…*again*.

"Well, that explains it," he said, his expression full of shock.

"Explains what?"

"Why I couldn't figure out why Dee never mentioned you having a baby." He snickered.

"She never mentioned Dallas? But I sent her pictures."

"Oh, she mentioned something all right." Bain was amused. "She talked about how you liked to dress up your...*cat*."

"Cat?" Fifi gasped, pulling Dallas closer as if to spare his feelings. "But she saw pictures. I sent them to her...*often*."

"Yeah," he went on, taking a jab now that he knew the property was being sold, "she always went on about how you dressed it up in these ridiculous outfits. She said you had a big heart, had to in order to love such an *ugly cat*."

"Dallas is *not* ugly. And clearly not a *cat*!" Fifi was offended.

Bain shook his head. "Nope...that there is definitely *not* a *cat*!"

"Dallas is a *sloth*!" Fifi defended.

"Of course he is. Hollywood didn't affect you one bit... pet sloths are totally normal." Bain sneered. "Anyway, can we talk about the property and maybe work something out?"

"Sure!" Fifi shrugged, grabbing what appeared to be a diaper bag before shutting the door and walking toward the house. "Make me an offer."

"An offer?" He followed. "Fine. I'll make you an offer. How about the six sides of beef, chicken coop, and freezer full of homemade casseroles I made last year. Think that'll cover it?"

She stopped abruptly. "People pay you with that stuff? What is this...Mayberry? How do you survive off that?"

"Some do because that's all they can pay. Not everything is about money, Fiona."

"It's Fifi, and casserole doesn't pay bills or put gas in the car, Jensen Bain."

"Look, I can't afford what this place is worth. Would you consider leasing part out — both parts, maybe? Perhaps turn it into a vacation rental, you know, an income property," he pleaded.

"One, I don't have the time to manage something like that, and I don't want strangers destroying my grandmother's house—"

"No, you'll just sell it to one," he added. "I could…you know, help manage it. Take that off your plate. I'm always here anyway and do most of the upkeep. It really wouldn't be that much, and I'll continue paying rent on my part—"

"All I hear is *liability, buffalo bite, lawsuit.* Look. I get it. You weren't expecting this, and it puts you in a bad spot."

"A bad spot? You're not only taking away the sanctuary of several animals but also taking away my business and my home. Surely, we can come up with some kind of arrangement. It won't be easy to find somewhere to move all this to."

"I agree. It probably won't. How about this…" she said as if she were offering him the deal of a lifetime. "How about you stay until it sells, and I'll add an extra thirty days to whatever sales agreement comes my way. That will buy you an extra month beyond the purchase to find somewhere else for your…zoo."

"Thirty days. Thirty days? This is prime real estate in a highly sought-after vacation destination. It won't be on the market more than a week. If not a developer, some investor will swoop in and turn it into the very vacation rental I suggested."

"Well, maybe the new owner will like the idea of a zoo at

his or her investment property. I'll be sure to introduce you so you can pitch the idea."

"Nobody is going to go for that."

"Exactly. And neither am I. This place..." She looked around. "It holds some of my fondest childhood memories... all of them, really. I loved it here. It was so magical then. But with Gram gone and my life back in LA...I just don't see how keeping it makes sense. I'm really sorry. I'll be here this week to get it ready, but it's going on the market."

2

"Not agaaain," Fifi whined at the sound of the doorbell. "How on earth do they know I'm here? It's only eight in the morning."

At seven sharp, Fifi's doorbell rang, and had been going off every few minutes since with no end in sight. Each time she answered, a stranger was on the other side with a friendly smile, some sympathetic words about the late Dee Gallagher, and a plated dish of sorts. She had a dozen casseroles, a few meat and cheese trays, a Jell-O ring with some concoction in it, and a bowl of fruit. There were a few bouquets of fresh flowers in the mix, but it was mostly a whole lot of carbs keeping her from falling back into a restful slumber.

This time, however, when she opened the door, her smile was a little less forced. The immediate aroma of fresh pastries tickled her senses and riled her memories. She knew what was in the pink pastry box with the Baker's Bakery logo on top. Her stomach rumbled at the sweet smell of her childhood favorite, apple fritters — what Jed Baker was best known for. With a quick thanks, she pulled a fritter out and tossed the box on the table with all the other food.

"It's still warm," she said to herself. "This is worth every last gram of gluten."

"Mmm…" Her eyes all but rolled back in her head as she fell against the wall, enjoying the nostalgia. "It's been years since I've had anything this good."

It *had* been years. Growing up, Fifi had only lived a handful of hours away in Portland, so it was easy to spend summers with her grandmother. When her father passed, her mother, a writer, moved them to Los Angeles for a new start and never looked back. Fifi, then Fiona, had only been fourteen the last time she'd visited. After that, her grandmother flew out to see her in LA each summer, but that only lasted for a few years. The travel became harder on Dee, and Fifi's schedule grew as fast as she did.

Being in McKenzie Ridge again was bittersweet. It *was* full of *nostalgia*. She'd felt it the minute she'd arrived, but those memories were accompanied with guilt over time lost — or time she hadn't made for her grandmother. Phone calls each week just hadn't been the same as spending time with her grandmother in that place. She knew that now, of course, and wished she could go back and do things differently. Fifi had thought she'd had time.

As much as the memories wandering the house made her happy, they also reminded her why she couldn't stay and why she needed to sell the property. It had been a happy place as a child, but as an adult, it was a total inconvenience. She'd become accustomed to the city life, where everything she needed or wanted was easy to get to.

In McKenzie, she couldn't even get takeout delivered unless she wanted to order from Ponderosa Pizza, and that was only if the pimple-faced teen with the beat-up Volkswagen Bug was working as the part-time, once-in-a-while *delivery kid*. Well, unless you happened to call when a nearby neighbor was dining in and willing to swing by to drop off your order on their way home. Otherwise, you drove a few miles into town to grab what you needed, and at that point, you might as well have stayed and eaten while it was fresh and warm.

They didn't even have grocery delivery or a real dry cleaner. The dry cleaner was a guy who did your clothes on the side out of the back of his seasonal vacation tour business. It was a tourist town, busy every season, but what kept people coming back was the quaint, simple charm. Fifi didn't do quaint — or simple.

Another knock on the door pulled Fifi from her wandering thoughts and left her licking her sticky fingers as she made her way to whoever was on the other side, hoping they had a nice platter of bean dip. It was five o'clock somewhere, and if you could drink at that hour, you could have bean dip too.

The knocking persisted, louder and more insistent. "I'm coming, I'm coming, geez!"

Annoyed by the urgent sympathizer on her step, Fifi flung the door open. "What do you want...?"

She paused at the familiar face, taking a minute to place it. She knew those kind eyes and that warm smile. "You," Fifi said.

"Yeah, well, you too," the older woman said, pushing right past Fifi with a chuckle that could belong to only one person.

"That fresh mountain air makin' you feel a little funny? That's just the stink air you're used to breathin' leavin' your system."

"Lou Shaw?" Fifi asked, watching the woman make her way to the kitchen. "I...I'm—"

"I know, I know...sorry for acting so Hollywood with

your rude greeting," the woman said. "And since when do you call me Lou Shaw? Jesus, you've been drinkin' already? It ain't but eight or nine in the mornin'. Unless it's one of those fancy LA drinks with the orange juice and champs, you ought to at least wait till 'round noon, or you'll build yourself a reputation."

Lou plopped a large bag on the counter, reached into her purse, and pulled out a flask, tossing back a healthy-size swig. "Now, you get yourself one of these and tell everyone it's medicinal. That's how you do your drinkin' before lunch."

"Uh…come in?" Fifi said sarcastically, shutting the door so she could follow Lou.

"Well, I already did, darlin'. You feelin' all right? Got yourself a little bit of that jet lag?"

"Jet lag doesn't work that way. Besides, I drove." Fifi chuckled.

"Ah. So that ridiculous tin can in the driveway is yours then." Lou nodded, piecing things together.

Fifi gasped. "Tin can? That *expensive luxury* car cost me a fortune."

"Expensive? Maybe. But luxury will have you in a ditch on these gravel roads this time of year or in a snowbank in the winter. Fancy don't do well in McKenzie, honey."

Louise Shaw was like McKenzie Ridge royalty. Everyone knew her, most liked her, some respected her, but all feared her and her cantankerous ways — in the best possible way, of course. Lou Shaw was always good-intentioned even when she meddled. Fifi smiled. Some things just didn't change, and it seemed Lou was one of those things. Somehow, that was comforting.

"Wh-What are you doing here?" Fifi asked, leaning to one side to see what Granny Lou had in her large cross-body bag she was wearing. "Did your bag just…*move*?"

"Oh," she said, patting the side, "this here's Whiskey. He's my dog. Just have him out for a walk. Ole Doc Bain says he's a little…hefty and needs some exercise."

A small black and gray dapple color head that didn't match the proportion of the size of the bag popped out, and one blue and one green eye stared back at Fifi. "If you're carrying him, how is he getting any exercise?"

"Well, I'm walkin' him," Lou said matter-of-factly. "You lose some sense out there in Holly-weird?"

Lou shook her head and began to unpack the bag she'd put on the counter. "I thought it best he be protected in the event you brought that cat Dee told us all about."

"I don't have a cat." Fifi snorted.

"Sure ya do. Dee showed us. Ugly gus if you ask me, but looks aren't everything, I s'pose."

"Dallas is actually a…uh, *sloth*," Fifi said.

"A what? What the hell is a sloth?"

"Well, it's an exotic animal. Cute as can be. And easy to take care of because they're always right where you leave them." Fifi shrugged. She briefly stepped out of the room, then returned with Dallas on her hip.

"Well, I'll be damned. I thought those were just made up and in children's books or somethin'," Lou hooted. "Still ugly, though. Anywho, we have time to work on replacin' that car of yours before winter. It's just nice to have ya back with us."

"Oh, I won't be here for winter," Fifi was quick to answer.

"Oh, darlin', you got a lot to relearn 'bout these mountains," Lou tsk'd. "Winter ain't always the best time to vacation, might get snowed *out* as easily as you can get snowed *in*."

"I mean, I won't be here because I'm not staying. I could

never live here. I'm selling the property and heading back to LA later in the week," Fifi assured.

"Selling it? But Dee always thought you'd take over here. That's all you talked about growin' up…livin' in McKenzie. It wouldn't be the same with anyone but Dee or you living here. It would change the whole town."

"The whole town? That's sweet you thought so highly of my gram. She really was the best."

"One of a kind," Lou agreed.

"Exactly. But I'm sure the town will get along just fine with someone else living here."

"I don't think you understand," Lou went on. "What about the Christmas festival?"

Fifi shrugged. "What about it?"

"Well, who will run it?" Lou's voice raised an octave. "After what happened this past winter, our Christmas festival was moved to July so the town could be restored first."

McKenzie Ridge had been through a terrible tragedy just before the holidays when someone who didn't belong came to town and burned much of it to the ground in the name of revenge. In true McKenzie fashion, the town came together, rebuilt, and planned to have their annual Christmas festival just the same…even if it had to be in July.

"Uh…whoever ran it before?" Fifi wasn't sure why they were playing this game, but if she remembered anything about Lou Shaw, it was that she was always up to something.

"That was Dee," Lou informed.

Fifi paused. Of course it was her grandmother. She should have known that since Christmas *was* her favorite time of year. "Maybe skip a year? Find someone else to do it? I mean, it's already July and Christmas is right around the corner again. Why not just…wait?"

"I'd agree with ya, except…it was Dee who insisted we

still have our Christmas. She said somethin' about risin' from the ashes — literally — like that bird or what have ya," Lou pleaded.

"A phoenix." Fifi smiled. "Rise like a phoenix from the ashes. I think that was her favorite advice to give."

"Yeah, I just remembered the damn bird. Anywho… doesn't her insistence kind of make this here festival her dyin' wish? Maybe that's where you fit in to all of this?"

There it was again, that sense of looming guilt Fifi had been wearing since she'd received the dreaded phone call.

"Me?" Fifi dramatically pointed at herself. "Oh no…"

"Now, hear me out." Lou continued. "Maybe you're supposed to carry out her wish and run one last festival…in her honor."

"Surely there's someone else," Fifi reasoned.

"Sure. There's a gang of volunteers, but your gram was the magic."

"I don't have her magic, Granny Lou."

"Oh, but you do. Dee talked about it all the time — how creative and successful you are — and that you're an artist."

"I wouldn't know the first thing about planning a town festival."

Lou snorted. "Sure ya would! Treat it like one of your movie sets. Dee always talked about how she'd taken a tip or two from your sets. Oh, and look for the notebook. She kept everything in that old tattered thing. The festival is only a few weeks away, right after the Fourth of July festival."

"Wait, there's a Fourth of July festival immediately followed by a…Christmas festival?"

Lou gave Fifi another one of those cross looks. "Well, that's what I said, honey. You needin' a nap already?" Lou reached out and placed the back of her hand on Fifi's forehead. "No fever, so it must be fatigue."

And just like that, Lou was headed for the front door as if the decision had been made. "I'll be back at nine sharp tomorrow morning with the others to help you set up. Most of the committee will be there. It might be nice to have a little chat on the side and get morale up."

"Set up what? Here?" Fifi wasn't sure what had just happened, but suddenly, it didn't feel like she was headed back to LA at the end of the week. She didn't bother to address the festival comment as it seemed less urgent now.

"The party!" Lou said as if Fifi's question was absurd. "You sure you're feelin' all right? Everyone will be here tomorrow for a final goodbye."

"Wait. Gram's will says no funeral."

Lou shook her head. "It's going to take a bit to get you back into the swing of things around here, I see. We aren't havin' a funeral. No one wants to be stuck in a box with a bunch of crybabies hanging over their hole in the ground. We throw goin' away parties. Think of it as a memorial, but fun."

"Well, isn't all that the same thing? A funeral and a memorial?" Fifi asked.

"Not even close. Funerals are depressing. Our parties are fun, and we get to drink a little."

"Why wouldn't my gram say she wanted—?"

Lou cut her off, "Honey, none of us put it in writing. We're old, not shallow. No one ever asks for a surprise party, do they?"

"This is hardly a surprise party. She passed away over a month ago while I was out of the country for work. What's there to celebrate about that?"

"Was your gram's passin' a surprise?" Lou questioned.

"Of course. Out of the blue."

"Did she live a good life, treat people right, and laugh a bit?"

"Yes to all of those things."

"Well, then…it's worth celebrating. We're havin' a party. It's just a known thing around here. We don't ask for our movin' on party. Those left behind just throw them." Lou winked.

"But if not for you, I wouldn't have known. Are you sure this is the right thing to do? I really don't want to go against her wishes."

"That's what the committee is for," Lou answered.

"A committee?" Fifi was shocked. "Do you guys have a committee for everything around here?"

With a proud smile as she was the head of most town committees, Lou said, "Just about! Things run smoother when you have a committee overseeing things."

Fifi stood in awe. This little town was more organized and busier than the multimillion-dollar productions she worked on — and that was saying something. "Well, I was going to start going through things so I could get the house on the market, but I guess I'm going to the store for party food."

"Food?" Lou looked around Fifi at the table covered in food dishes. "What do you think all the casseroles and food trays are for?"

Fifi glanced at the buffet she'd been acquiring all morning, "I just thought…Let me guess, that was part of the committee?"

"Now you're gettin' it. See, McKenzie's in your blood. I knew it would start to come back to ya." Lou chuckled. "That was the catering committee droppin' by all morning. They handle all the births, sicknesses, and deaths. They make sure everyone is fed in their time of need."

"Of course there's a committee for that." Fifi laughed. "I guess I shouldn't have dug into that taco casserole then. I know it was early, but it looked good."

"Don't eat another bite. That ain't taco casserole," Lou scolded.

"What is it then?"

"That's the thing, no one really knows, but cream of broccoli soup should never be in the same dish as pico de gallo and pickles. All we know is if ya eat it, you get the sceamin' mimis for days," Lou said in a near whisper as if someone would overhear. "If ya know what I mean."

"I think I know what you mean by the screamin'…well, ya know. I thought it was odd to have a clove and cinnamon after taste. I'll just throw it out."

"You'll do no such thing. We ain't in the business of hurtin' people's feelin's. Feelin's may not matter out there in your fancy city, but they do here."

"But if it makes people sick…"

"Everyone knows Mrs. Tilly's hearts in the right place. She just can't cook a lick. We just take out a scoop and set it out, and when she goes to see how her dish is fairin', she's pleased to see it's being eaten — or so she thinks. It's the neighborly thing to do."

"Why not just tell her—?"

"Oh, Fiona." Lou shook her head. "Do you want to be the one to tell her that her cookin' is more dangerous than a hand grenade in a propane tank?"

"A what?" Fifi put her hands out to halt a response. "Never mind. I get it. We let her think it's a hit and burn it later. And it's actually Fifi now."

Lou patted Fifi on the shoulder. "See, you're already fittin' right back in, *Fiona*."

Lou jaunted out the door, hollering over her shoulder, "See ya tomorrow, bright and early."

3

"I SEE THE CATERING COMMITTEE HAS BEEN HERE ALREADY," Bain said, coming in the back door. "They went all out. Brought flowers too. Wow."

Fifi turned to face him, tossing a thumb over her shoulder in the direction of the door. "Something just happened. I have no idea what, but I think I'm throwing a surprise party for my late gram, and I'm now the chairperson of the Christmas festival that happens immediately after the...Fourth of July festival?"

"I thought that was Lou's truck out there." He laughed. "Didn't take her long at all."

"Are we trapped in a bad episode of that old show? This is really starting to feel like Mayberry."

Bain shrugged his shoulders. "Close. Just real-life McKenzie Ridge. It's all a part of the charm. They all mean well."

"Yeah, I don't know why I thought it'd be any different. Gram always talked about the community and how it was like a big family. I guess I'd forgotten just how true that was because she was *not* wrong."

"Your gram did love this town and all the things that made it special, like that Christmas festival. I think she always saw you as part of it…you know, someday," Bain said.

"Yeah." Fifi paused, distracted by that thought. There was a time when she also saw herself in McKenzie. Somewhere along the way, though, everything changed. Her goals, dreams, everything. "We would talk about it. I guess I didn't realize how serious she took it. I mean, as a little girl, all I wanted was to live here with my gram. As I got older, it all sort of changed. We still talked about it, but it was more out of habit for me, something to keep her happy."

"And now you regret it," Bain finished for her.

"A little bit. I feel bad that she was creating this grand legacy, or so it seems, to leave me because she thought I wanted it. I guess I led her on a bit," Fifi admitted. She wasn't sure why she was confiding in Jensen Bain. It just came easily. "I do wish I had visited more, though."

"I'm sorry," he said.

"For what?"

"For…LA." Bain shrugged.

Fifi was starting to remember why this guy rubbed her the wrong way. "I happen to love LA."

"I don't."

She didn't care even a little bit about Dr. Jensen Bain, but he had her curious, so she followed him out the back door. "You've been there?"

"I was born and raised in Los Angeles," Bain deadpanned. He stopped on the deck and turned to face her. "Everyone in my family is a vet. It's sort of in our blood. I started my own practice there. Did well, actually. The people there love their expensive trophy pets and are willing to pay a pretty penny. So much so, when my brother was ready to start practicing medicine, he bought my clinic, and I was able to move here and live a good life making next to nothing."

When Doc Bain turned to continue in the direction he intended, Fifi was on his heels. "You left LA for *this*? *How*? *Why*? I just don't get it."

"Because here I'm actually living, Fiona. In California, I was just working, trying to make the next buck, and I didn't even know what I was working for. Here...I do."

Something about the doc's statement was profound and stood out to Fifi. She understood the long hours focused only on work. When she really thought about it, all she did was work. Sure, there was the occasional night out with friends at a swanky LA hot spot...but it was usually work-related. She could count on her hand how many times she'd been to the beach, and most trips were also work-related. Fifi was living all right — living to work.

"Well, I guess I'll get to see what that whole living thing is like since I'll be here a while — until the end of the Christmas festival Lou Shaw weaseled her way into making me in charge of."

Doc stopped in his tracks. Though he wouldn't admit it, hearing Fifi was staying caused a twinge in his gut he hadn't felt in some time.

"Really? You think you can handle *Mayberry* for that long, Fiona?"

She shrugged. "With a little wine, I can do anything. They do sell that here, don't they?"

"Some of the best wine to cross your palette is from right here in McKenzie. Morgan Jameson has an award-winning boutique wine from the vines on her ranch."

"Now, that's a name I haven't heard in a while. I remember the Jameson ranch. I suppose I'll have to see what this fancy mountain wine of hers is all about," Fifi said. "I think the extra time will be helpful. I can really get things in order around here and maybe work on my passion project a little. Somehow, I feel a little inspired here, which is completely blowing me away."

Bain started to walk off again. Mention of the house being sold dulled that twinge he was nurturing. "Right. The house. Need to sell it because...LA."

"It's where my job is, Jensen. My whole life."

"Really? What's this passion project of yours? What is this place *inspiring*, Fiona?"

Put off by the sharpness to his tone, she matched it with her own sass. "Not that it's any of your business, but I've been writing. I'd like to finish, publish, and option to a production company. And it's Fifi...*not* Fiona."

Bain hadn't seen that coming. Dee had mentioned how creative Fiona was, that she was talented, and that that talent was being wasted. She'd said no matter how many awards her granddaughter won or how successful she was at what she did, nothing topped her real talent, which must've been writing.

"I'll let you get back to selling your grandmother's house. Enjoy that passion project. It's a real shame you want to get rid of your inspiration, though. And it's *Bain*, or *Doc Bain*. Nobody calls me *Jensen*." Two could play this game, he thought.

Unsure why she was still following him, Fifi fired back, "Yeah, well at least my passion pays me in real money and not chickens."

"That's really great for you, *Fifi*. But something tells me you don't really know what your passion is. And if it's reserved as a *project*, maybe you should rethink your priorities. Just my two cents, but I think you have a *job* because you're afraid to live your *passion*. But what do I know? I get paid in chickens." He shrugged and walked away once again.

Determined to get the last word, she was right back on his heels, but before she followed him off the back deck, she was stopped dead in her tracks and screamed as she fell backward. She scooted away as fast as she could because one of the barn cats dropped a dead blackbird at her feet.

Only a few paces ahead of her, Doc turned and kneeled in front of her, his hands on her shoulders before she could catch her breath. "What? Fiona, what is it? Are you okay? Did you fall?"

She shook her head violently and pointed toward the bird. "Your...cat. It...it killed a bird. Why would it do that? Why would it kill a bird and put it at my feet like that?"

Bain laughed, crisis averted. He rolled to his side, taking a seat next to her. "It's a gift. They do that. In fact, I'm surprised ole Missy has that left in her."

"Missy? *That* was Missy?" Fifi questioned. "I...I found her during my last summer here."

"I know. Dee told me she was your cat," Bain said. "She told me you two were inseparable, and the day you left was the day Missy became a barn cat. Hasn't been inside since."

"Really? Why wouldn't Gram tell me that? She hasn't mentioned Missy in so long, I thought she'd passed or run off."

"Maybe your gram was starting to figure out this place didn't really mean as much to you as it once had when *you* stopped asking about the things you once cared about." Bain took to his feet and headed for the barn. "My guess is Missy remembers exactly who you are, and that bird was a welcome home gift...animals in the mountains don't do diamonds like LA cats."

Fifi stood. "Do you have any *normal* animals around here?"

"You mean, like a sloth?" Bain fired back over his shoulder. "We're fresh out. They all moved to LA."

4

Right on time, Lou Shaw showed up as promised with an army of help to set up for Dee Gallagher's...*party*.

"Be a dear and run out to the barn and grab the extra folding tables," Lou said to Fifi. "That handsome doc can show you where they are. Expectin' a big crowd for Dee today."

Fifi smiled and nodded, heading for the back door. Distracted by guilt and a man who kept wedging his way under her skin — in a bad way — she hadn't really had time to process her grandmother's passing, and this *party* was forcing her to deal with the grief.

The distractions, however, were wearing thin. There wasn't enough wine to numb the pain, and there was the whole part about being a sober party host. Dee was all Fifi really had because once her dad had died, her mother was never the same. Though she didn't see her grandmother and their relationship was strictly through weekly phone calls, it was something. And that something was gone.

"Hey," Fifi said with a weak voice, grabbing Doc's attention. "Lou sent me to ask for the folding tables you keep out here."

Doc's expression softened when he noticed her somber, almost sad, look. "Uh. Yeah, I don't know why she sent you clear out here. They're up by the house in the shed."

"Weird. Lou said *the handsome doc...*" Fifi looked at her feet and chuckled. "Never mind. I think we have a matchmaker on our hands."

Doc matched her laugh. "Yeah, sounds about right."

"Wait. You're not mad?" Fifi asked.

"I'm used to it. My guess is she's on double duty, filling in for your grandmother, thinking she's doing her a favor by trying to marry you off to the rich in chicken doctor."

"Excuse me? I'm perfectly capable of finding my own... whatever," Fifi defended.

"So, you have someone? Back home?" Doc asked.

"Well, no...I just mean I could if I wanted to. You know, on my own."

"Of course you could." Doc tried to smooth over the wedge building between them. "That's what the *senior crowd* does around here. They don't mean any harm. I mean, what's it hurt to let a couple of old ladies think they're doing something nice and helpful? They've been trying to set me up since I landed here a decade ago."

"I'm only here a few weeks, so I guess it doesn't matter." Fifi shrugged. "So, you've been here and single the whole time?"

"Nooo, not the whole time. I was actually engaged for a while." He motioned for her to follow him. "I'll help you get the tables out of the shed."

Fifi went quietly. The silence between them was deafening, and it was all she could do not to ask what had happened to the fiancée. It didn't make an ounce of sense why she wanted to know so bad...or why the idea of a fiancée had her feeling a bit jealous. She didn't like the man. He was moody, worked for food instead of cash, and cared more about animals than people. What did all that say about a person anyway? *Sure*, she thought, *you could call that charitable and kind, but his mood is unpredictable and rude.* Or was it just that she stormed in here and told him she was selling his home? It didn't matter either way. He didn't matter in the grand scheme of things because she was leaving.

But, her business or not, what did she have to lose?

"So, what happened?" she asked.

"To what?" he asked.

"Your fiancée?" Fifi asked quietly, broaching the subject carefully.

"Oh. Yeah, that." He chuckled, turning his gaze to her. "She moved to LA."

There it was. No wonder he was salty about her and LA. She was like a slap in the face, another hit from LA. First his girl, and now his home. It was adding up.

Doc reached the shed and pulled on the partially open double doors. "They're over here in the corner."

Fifi followed him in — and promptly ran out screaming.

"It's okay, Timber. She's friendly. She won't hurt you," Doc hollered at the wild turkey giving chase.

"Are you kidding me?" Fifi yelled, running right back to the shed to hide behind Doc. "I won't hurt *him*?"

Doc laughed with a shrug. "He has trust issues. Go on, Timber. Get out of here. You know better than to be in here anyway."

Doc clapped his hands after the turkey, sending him in a different direction while Fifi ducked back in the shed to catch her breath.

"Sorry about that," Doc said, popping back in. "He gets in

the damnedest places."

Fifi watched the turkey wander off, walking in an odd circle as he did. "What's wrong with it?"

"He has a short wing. The others picked at him because he was *different.* Animals do that kind of thing until they kill off the outsider. So, he lives here, though I don't know why he's always walking in circles. Best I can come up with is that bum wing throws off his balance, and he's always leanin' that way. Nothing medical to explain otherwise."

"Wow," Fifi said, her demeanor suddenly sympathetic. "That's actually really sad. They picked at him because he was…*different*? Maybe animals aren't much different than humans after all."

Fifi propped her elbow on the shelf beside her, watching the odd-looking turkey wander off. A hissing sound quickly followed, causing her to scream once again. When Fifi backed away from its source, she tripped over her own feet and fell right into Doc Bain's strong arms.

"Whoa." He said, "I gotcha. Nothing to be afraid of. Just ole Maude."

"Who?" Fifi screeched as Doc lifted her to her feet, arms still around her.

"Maude. She's an opossum."

"Are you kidding me? I was almost bit! That thing could have rabies."

"First things first, all my animals are treated and vaccinated by me," Bain said, completely offended. "And second, I've had her since she was a baby. No idea what happened to her family. She was loose in town, sick, and scared. I took her in, fixed her up, treated a massive infection that cost her all of her teeth, and she's been with me ever since. Can't really survive in the wild without teeth."

"No teeth?" Fifi looked closer, earning another hiss as the opossum scurried off.

"Nope. I feed her soft cat food. She and Timber are their own pack and always together."

"A wild turkey and an opossum. Isn't one nocturnal and one…not nocturnal?" Fifi asked. "I mean, I'm sure I learned that somewhere."

"Yep. Somehow they make it work between them." Doc shrugged. "All the animals around here do."

Noticing his hands still firmly around her waist, she pulled away and remembered she was mad at him for one reason or another. "Well, maybe we should keep things locked up around here, and perhaps I can get a list of animals so I don't get spooked by a llama or stray grizzly."

"I purposely keep things unlocked because they'll find a way in regardless," Doc defended. "I check all the outbuildings and anywhere else these guys can get themselves trapped every night to make sure everyone is fed for the day and accounted for."

As much as Fifi wanted to admire Doc's commitment to the animals, she didn't. "Well, then maybe the list…and how about you keep your hands to yourself."

"Right. Next time, I'll let you fall on your *ass*." Doc grabbed a folding table under each arm and charged past her. "I'll work on your *list*, but maybe you could just walk around clapping your hands and whistling to shoo out any animals in your path in the meantime."

"Wait!" she yelled after him. "Is that a thing, or are you just trying to make me look as ridiculous as your bum animals clapping and whistling."

"It's not the animals who are ridiculous right now, *Fiona*."

5

The number of people filtering in and out of Fifi's grandmother's house was impressive. She knew her grandmother had been well-liked, but it seemed the whole town had stopped by to share their condolences and sweet stories about Dee Gallagher. Many of them were like Dee, longtime McKenzie residents who had fond memories Fiona was even a part of. She felt closer to her grandmother than she had in years, despite her absence.

Though her guilt was heightened as she realized just how much she'd missed over the years, her heart was still full. Fifi was proud to be Dee Gallagher's granddaughter. The idea of an extended stay in this town with these people didn't seem nearly as daunting as it originally had. The more she reminisced and got reacquainted, the more she felt inspired too. When she wasn't working on the biggest festival the town hosted, she spent her time writing. It was a good plan and, if she was honest with herself, a much-needed break from her typically busy life.

"Yes, Mr. Bentley. I completely understand your committee deserves a voice and float in the parade too," Fifi went on, feeling like a broken record. "Like I said, noon at the Ponderosa. We'll talk over pizza."

What Mr. Bentley didn't know was the meeting he just confirmed with Fifi to discuss his concerns included every other committee head who had approached her that day. It seemed the committees were fighting, and she was their mediator. What better way to do so than have them all agree to a sit-down without even knowing?

"This is like small-town mafia stuff," she said to herself, looking for a bottle of wine to fill her glass. "All the mob bosses in one place to discuss turf in the parade and festival…"

"You okay?" Bain asked with a concerned look. "Talking to yourself in the corner with a bottle of wine in one hand and empty glass in the other might make you tomorrow's talk of the town."

"Yeah. I hadn't thought of that." Fifi chuckled, handing him the bottle. "I just can't wrap my mind around how the smallest things are the big things around here. Did you know the various committees are holding their contributions hostage until they get things like a generator for their float or the corner booth they've been waiting years for during the festival?"

"Oh yeah. They take this stuff seriously." Bain laughed, filling his own glass. "And they have no shame hitting you up at Dee's party."

"Yeah, well I think they each think they're being clever and that the others wouldn't have the nerve to do so," Fifi said. "I'm onto them, though. Want to know a secret?"

Bain leaned in.

"I have them all meeting me at the Ponderosa to talk out details. All of them. Same time. Same place. And none of them know the others will be there."

"Smart," Bain said, impressed by how quickly Fifi was catching on. "That's something right out of Dee's book. Guess the apple doesn't fall far from the tree."

"Really?" Fifi smiled. "Thank you. I always wanted to be as great as her one day."

"I think you already are." Bain's expression went from playful to serious. "She'd be proud of you. I mean, she already was. You were all she talked about, but this…" He waved his arms around. "This is next level, Dee Gallagher style. It says something that the people are already coming to you, and you've been in town, what…three days?"

Fifi nodded with a smile while taking in the room. Thinking back to all the conversations she'd had with her grandmother as she shared the trivial things she'd been tasked with doing, the small-town gossip and shenanigans, the ridiculous feuds that would last a day, maybe two — it was satisfying to be in the presence of all the things that made her grandmother who she was. Fifi was flattered that the townspeople were already looking at her as the next Gallagher in charge. Leaving it all behind would be hard.

"Whatcha doin' over there all alone, honey?" Granny Lou asked, pulling Fifi from her thoughts.

Fifi hadn't noticed Doc had moved on, working the room. Her gaze roamed, knowing just where to find him. It always did. He was infuriating, but something else about him had her attention.

"Fiona, honey?" Lou said as she approached, reaching for Fifi's forehead, which seemed to be her response to everything. "You feelin' all right? Is this too much for you? Or have you just been hittin' that wine bottle a little hard?" Her voice dropped to a whisper. "It's okay. I won't tell anyone if you like the *bottle* a little bit."

"No, I'm fine." Fifi giggled. "I'm just…impressed. I'm overwhelmed by how much my gram was liked."

"Loved, you mean. Dee Gallagher was the heart and soul of this town," Lou said. "And it seems they're takin' to you just as fondly, dear. I heard about the meetin's…at the Ponderosa?"

Fifi's eyes widened. "Crap. They know I set them all up?"

"Nooo, honey. I'm just sharper than a whip and put it all together. All these jabber jaws spillin' their news like they just won the war and don't have a clue you set them all up to battle it out face-to-face. Classic Dee Gallagher move. She'd be impressed," Lou said with an approving wink.

"So I hear," Fifi said.

"Oh. So that's what that handsome doc was over here tellin' ya." Lou looked over her shoulder before pulling her flask from her oversized purse and taking a quick swig. "I thought there was somethin' between the two of ya."

"Oh, no. Nothing like that." Fifi waved her hands in front of her, fearing the misconception would spread if she didn't kill it now. "We barely get along. He's so—"

"Literal, down to earth, laid-back, easygoing, handsome," Lou said, finishing Fifi's thoughts.

"Well, yes…most of that. And I'm so—"

"Uptight, rigid, bossy, in denial—"

"Yes. I mean no! I mean…I'm just focused, have a plan, and have a life to get back to," Fifi defended. "We don't mix. Like oil and vinegar. Fire and ice."

"Sometimes those things go together more than you think," Lou pointed out. "Like oil and vinegar make a nice dressing, and fire and ice…well, have you ever had a shot of fireball on the rocks? It'll knock your socks off."

Fifi responded with a confused look. "Actually, I haven't."

"Well, then that's your problem. You need to let that tight, stick-up-your-ass bun on top of your head loose and let your hair down and give your cheekbones a rest. Live a little while you're here. It just might change your life."

"My what?" Fifi patted her hair, suddenly self-conscious.

"That hairdo. You got it pulled so tight that your cheekbones are like razor blades. I'm surprised your damn eyeballs haven't fallen out." Lou took another hit from the flask. "Look around. Notice anything? And since you're a little slow at this, bein' from the city, look at the hairdos."

Fifi scanned the crowd and noticed quite a few tightly slicked-back buns in the crowd, but she didn't understand the significance.

"Ever since your cheekbones arrived, the ladies have all been pulling their hair back as tight as they can. They call it the Fifi lift."

"The what?"

"Smooths out the wrinkles, darlin'. It's like a face-lift but without the knife." Lou laughed. "Their breasts are swingin' to their knees and they have saggy rumps, but their faces are nice and tight. You're the new fashion icon around here."

"Oh? Ohhhh." With a little heads-up, Fifi saw it clear as day. "I had no idea."

"Your grandmother always talked so highly of you and your glamorous life…these old bats have been watching you since the day you arrived." Lou chuckled.

"But I haven't been anywhere."

"You don't have to go anywhere. It's McKenzie, and news travels fast. All it took was dropping a few dishes by yesterday to see what *glamour* looks like. Now, you're trending."

"Oh, this is so embarrassing. I…" Fifi stammered. "I don't even know what to say. I only put my hair up because something about this dry mountain air makes my hair frizzy and full of static."

"Is that all?" Lou snorted. "All you need to do is rub your hair with a dryer sheet. Problem solved."

"That's...gross."

"Is it? Why? If it's good enough for your clothes, it should be good enough for your hair, honey. Give it a whirl. Wear your hair down and see what happens."

"I don't know. That seems so—"

"Not hoity-toity Hollywood?" Lou winked. "You know who taught me that trick? Dee."

A group of ladies joined them before Fifi could reply with anything. What *was* there to say? Lou was sweet, thoughtful, and blunt as hell. Fifi's takeaway from the conversation thus far was that Lou and the others thought her life was as glamorous as it was...pretentious. Nothing like being put in your place, kindly, and told to relax. Maybe Lou was on to something.

"Look at these, honey," Lou said, taking a stack of pictures from one of the ladies who joined them. "These were from our ladies' retreat. Group of us went skinny dippin' up at the hot springs for a whole weekend."

"You what?" Fifi choked on her sip of wine. "You didn't really—"

"Go swimmin' in our birthday suits? Damn tootin' we did." Lou elbowed her gently. "When you get to our age, there ain't much ya haven't seen or done. No shame in bein' nude. Besides, the *girls* hang far enough down to cover the *hoo-has,* so we were still keepin' things...*private.*"

"Oh, my God. Now there's a visual I didn't need," Fifi said, stunned. "Please tell me there aren't any...*girls* or...*hoo-has* in these pictures."

"Oh, heavens no, our centerfold days are over, honey." Lou winked.

"Center…"

"She's kidding," one of the other ladies said. "None of us have done anything that scandalous unless you count that time Shirl accidentally video recorded herself in her skivvies on that FaceTime thing, and Peg accidentally sent it in one of those group things."

"It's called email, Percy," Lou said with an eye roll. "We call that the skivvy scandal because it certainly was that."

"Sounds pretty scandalous, all right." Fifi snickered. "You have to be careful with technology."

"Oh, that wasn't the scandal, honey." Lou shook her head. "Shirl had no business wearin' one of them thongs the young people wear. It was—"

"Scandalous?" Fifi laughed.

"Yes…" the ladies said in unison with a sigh and shake of the head at poor Shirl.

"Anywho, your gram was the best dressed of the bunch. We called her our fashionista," Lou said, flipping through the pictures. "She'd dress us all up in the things you'd send her. Said you sent it to be seen, and there was no reason to hide it in a closet. We were looking pretty sharp that weekend."

"Oh, my…" Fifi replied, taking a closer look. "I had no idea Jimmy Choo went with…flannel. And that…Swarovski handbag looks…mountain chic with those…hiking boots."

"Dee was sure proud of you. She showed you off any way she could. We were the flashiest bunch at the hot springs. People thought we were from your neck of the woods, I'm sure," Lou said.

"I can see…why." Fifi couldn't help but smile at Dee and her friends wearing full winter gear, surrounded by snow and pine trees, couture mixed with their plaid.

"She sure loved those big sparkle earrings. Wouldn't go to town without them or one of them fancy shoes," Lou said, stopping at a picture of just Dee. "Didn't have the heart to tell her she looked like a broke mountain hooker lookin' for milk money. Just ridiculous."

Fifi lost it in a fit of laughter. Lou Shaw called them as she saw them, and she wasn't wrong. Bright lipstick and all, Fifi adored the woman and missed her a little more with each picture as she discovered who Dee really was and realized she didn't get to know her the way she would have liked. Somehow, being around her friends and hearing their stories took the edge off that nagging guilt, leaving her with an odd sense of belonging.

* * *

Fifi laid in a hammock she'd been eyeing since she'd arrived. It rested far enough from the house to gain a little privacy as the crowd began to dwindle, and those who remained had shooed her off as they cleaned up the party and put things away. Fifi took in the expansive property around her. It amazed her how a crowd the size she'd hosted had managed to mingle, strange animals and all, like everything was normal. She figured this was normal for them. This was McKenzie in all its celebratory glory. A final farewell to one of their own with class and dignity. She rather liked it, even if she didn't like the circumstance that had brought them all together.

It was something she'd been missing and only just began to realize. Fifi summed it up to nostalgia, but she was beginning to remember what it was she loved so much about the place and why she wanted it to be home for so long...until she forgot what home was.

A gentle nudge and loud, screeching honk caused her to swing a little more aggressively than she'd prefer, and she nearly flipped when she caught herself, or rather, Doc Bain caught her.

"Whoa, Nelson," he said.

"What?"

"Well, you didn't scream this time." Bain laughed. "Look over your shoulder. And don't scream."

"Oh, hell. If it's a spider…" She panicked.

"Since when did you start swearing, and spiders make a sound like that?"

Fifi shrugged. "Since I spent time with Lou Shaw, wine, and all her *hoo-ha* talk. But so help me, if I turn around and get bit…"

"Then give me your hand, and I'll help you up," Bain said. "This isn't your hammock."

"Excuse me?"

He extended his hand, and she grabbed it. "You'll see in a second, Fifi."

When he pulled her to her feet, she quickly turned as if something was chasing her only to see a short, portly… donkey. It gimped around the side of the hammock and managed to curl up in it without incident.

"Um…" Fifi said. "Do I really want to know?"

"I guess I better finish working on that list for you," Bain teased, referring to the list of animals Fifi had requested. "That's Nelson. He's…a donkey."

"Yeah, I know what donkeys are. But why is he here and…in a hammock?"

"Well, I couldn't tell you why he's in the hammock. Dee put it up, went to pour herself a drink, came back, and there he was…in her hammock. It's been his ever since. His front right leg is shorter than the rest, born that way, so he trips a lot. I think that's why he prefers the hammock."

"That's actually really sad." Fifi reached her hand out, looking at Bain for permission before she pet Nelson. "He's very sweet."

"Good job, Nelson. You're the first one she's taken to. There may be hope yet," Bain jested.

Like a knife to the gut, his words were a sharp reminder not to get attached. She wasn't here for any reason other than business. She quickly pulled her hand away. "Leave it to you to ruin a moment. The only *hope* here is that the next few weeks pass by a little faster, and the house sells right away so I can be done with all this…mess."

And she stormed off.

Bain turned to the donkey with a shrug. "Guess I spoke too soon, buddy."

6

After a long day of hugging strangers, sharing stories, and remembering her grandmother, the house suddenly felt more empty than ever. Fifi was lonely. Maybe it was the finality of it all settling in, or the extensive amount of wine she'd spent the day with. Either way, she wasn't okay. With Dallas clinging to a nearby cat tree, Fifi decided to start looking for the mysterious notebook that supposedly contained everything she needed to know about the upcoming Christmas festival.

Dee was orderly, and everything had a place, but the most likely place didn't seem to have what she was looking for. The best Fifi could find was a calendar heavily coded in Christmas-like symbols, but nothing to decode it with. What each of those symbols stood for was anyone's guess.

Further digging and another bottle of wine later, she turned up totes with her name on them. Each one was full of keepsakes ranging from toddler-era art projects to memorabilia from Dee's trips to LA. Fifi's entire life with her grandmother had been preserved, unspoiled like some sort of time capsule. Rummaging through the totes was like a journey through her past, one memory after another. One smile after another.

For hours, Fifi rummaged through tote after tote, following the timeline of her life, never running low on wine as she did. The final tote was different. It didn't have as much in it, marking the time she left and never came back. She found ticket stubs from flights to LA accompanied by pictures and postcards her grandmother would pick up from the various tourist attractions they'd undoubtedly explore.

As the years went on, there were less art projects, fewer pictures, and no more plane tickets. Instead, there were magazine articles and old newspaper clippings where Fifi had been nominated for an award or won one. There were even ticket stubs to the movie theater one town over where Dee had watched a movie Fifi had worked on. A sob escaped her as she looked at their relationship and what it had become…in a scrapbook.

The guilt she'd been forcing down to deal with another time made its way to the surface, and it was slapping her square in the face. So many missed chances to share those experiences with her grandmother. She could have flown her out to accompany her to one of those movie premieres or awards shows, but Fifi had been too busy for even that. Instead, her grandmother's pride was so grand, she'd scrapbooked any morsel of Fifi's life she was allowed to be part of. It was limited to a small theater in a small mountain town just so she could see the sets Fifi designed…from a thousand miles away—just so she could feel close to her granddaughter.

Lou Shaw's previous words were starting to make sense. Fifi was pretentious, selfish really, and it was too late to do anything about it where Grandma Dee was concerned. That was a hard pill to swallow.

Bain walked in to see Fifi in the middle of the floor, closet door open, surrounded by its contents.

He set his plastic cup down and rushed to her side. "Are you okay? Fifi, are you hurt?"

She looked up at him, eyes swollen, and let out another sob. "No."

Pushing more of the debris around her to the side, he grabbed her hands, turning them top to bottom, inspecting her arms. Then he brushed a few loose strands of hair that had escaped her tight updo from her face before he cradled it, looking it over intently.

With one hand under her chin, he stroked her head, looking it over. "Was it your head? I don't see anything obvious. Help me out here. Where are you hurt, darlin'?"

With a pitiful whimper, she pointed at the center of her chest, and said, "Right here."

"Okay, honey. Let me see." Bain unbuttoned the top of her blouse and searched the area she'd pointed to. "I don't see anything here either. Were you hit very hard?"

When his large hand palmed her chest, her eyes closed. He slid from one side to the other, then out to her shoulders.

"I still don't feel or see anything wrong," he said. "I can't help you if you don't tell me where you're hurt, Fifi."

Another jerking sob. "My heart."

Panic crossed Bain's face as he quickly placed two fingers on Fifi's neck, searching for her pulse. "Everything...feels fine there too. Are you light-headed? Pain in your arm?"

"No, just a broken heart," Fifi cried.

"Broken?" Bain looked around the room again, the scene suddenly appearing different. "Did you...get this stuff out?"

She nodded.

He searched the items, trying to piece together whatever it was Fifi wasn't telling him. It didn't take long to see what everything had in common. It also didn't take long to notice the empty wineglass and matching bottle.

"I'm a terrible person," she slurred. "I was a terrible granddaughter. I was all she had left, and I was a...a...selfish asshole."

"No. Dee didn't see you that way," Bain said. "You were her pride and joy. I mean, look at this—"

"Mess!" Fifi said. "I made a damn frucking...*mess*."

"Wow. Wine makes you swear...sorta," Bain said. "I'll help you clean it up, then you can sleep it off and we'll talk tomorrow."

"Why are you being so nice to me? I have a stick up my ass and sharp cheekbones."

Bain gave her a side-eye glance. "Um, I'm not sure where that came from or what it means, but I'm being nice because—"

"You're a nice person. Lou told me you're nice, and I have a stick up my—" She gestured with her thumb, pointing up.

"Yeah, I get it. Uh-huh," Bain cut her off, minimizing her potential morning-after regrets. "Lou says a lot of things. You can't take her so literally. You're a good person, Fifi. Look around you. It was obvious how much you loved Dee."

"You just did it again," she said before another round of pouty tears. "You called me Fifi. See? So niiice."

"How about I help you put all this stuff back, and you can tell me about all of it as we put it away. Well...tell me as much as you remember," he teased.

"Drink with me?" she said, grabbing for the second bottle.

Bain intercepted. "I'll have a drink with you, but you have to let me pour. Deal?"

"Mm'kay. Fill'er up, Doc."

Bain reached for the plastic cup he'd set down when he

came in and poured himself some wine. He followed up with hers, pouring only a finger's worth. She was already feeling pretty good, or sad rather, and he didn't know how much she'd had to get there.

"You have more than me," she complained, comparing their glasses.

"No, you just have a bigger glass. It's even. Promise." It wasn't really lying if she wasn't sober. "Now, tell me everything there is to know about you growing up here in McKenzie and beyond."

Fifi hesitated at first, then watched Doc over the rim of her glass as she downed its contents. She extended her glass, and he poured the same amount.

"Your turn," she said as if it were a test.

Apparently, he passed because she picked up the item closest to her and gave it a story before they moved it back to its place in one of the bins. Hours passed, as did more than one bottle of wine, before the couple was sitting in the middle of the floor, everything tucked back where it belonged.

"I don't think you have a stick," Bain said. "That's my medical opinion. And I'm nice because…I like you. I liked you before I knew you because…Dee said I had to like you."

He paused and furrowed his eyebrows, confused by his own statement. He knew what he meant, but it hadn't come out as he'd intended. *Wine.*

"I like you too because I never knew you." Fifi shrugged, her expression matching his. "I mean, I like that I don't know you. Like, I like you. I like you to like me…"

"I have no idea what you just said." Bain laughed.

Fifi shrugged. "Neither do I."

The couple fell into a fit of laughter, falling to the floor where they each laid, side by side, staring at the ceiling.

"I don't drink wine," Bain said. "I remember why now."

"I love wine. And remember why too." She laughed.

Doc rolled to his side and faced her. "And why is that?"

Fifi lay still, eyes fixed on the ceiling as she thought out her answer. "Because it's good. It's refreshing. Because…"

"Because?" he coaxed.

She rolled to her side, only inches between them. "Because it means I'm relaxing. It means I'm taking a break from it all. Because I'm just being me."

Doc brushed a few loose hairs from her eyes. "I like you being you."

"Me too. There's something about this place…you…this *wine*."

She began to laugh.

"I like that sound," he said, his hand still stroking her face. "Your laugh…"

Her expression turned serious as she searched his eyes. "I like you too…"

Doc leaned in, his nose touching hers while he searched her eyes, waiting for permission to kiss her, when she pressed forward, kissing him instead. It was a gentle kiss, timid, unsure. When they pulled away, each smiled at the other, and their mouths found each other once more. Doc's hand drifted down her neck, to her shoulder and over the length of her, finally resting on her hip where he squeezed, earning a subtle moan.

With his hand on her ass, he pulled her body to his as the kiss they shared intensified and became so much more. Bain was gentle with her. Though his mind was fuzzy, he was aware they'd both been drinking and took things slow — until Fifi had other ideas.

In one swift motion, she pushed him to his back and straddled him, never losing their kiss. Bain's hands slid up her back, under her shirt, then back down again. Fifi joined him, moving against his motions, making his touch more intense. Her hands roamed under the hem of his T-shirt, letting out a breathy sigh when she felt the hard washboard beneath her touch. Doc Bain was hiding a well-chiseled physique.

Fifi sat up, catching her breath, her eyes still locked on Bain's. Slowly, she undid each button, one at a time, enjoying the flashes of mischief in his eyes as she did. When she dropped her blouse from her shoulders, letting it pool around her.

Bain's gaze drifted over her creamy skin, his hands following the view, touching every bare inch of her. Fifi arched as his hands grazed her sides, his nails just rough enough to leave a tingle she began to crave. Like a tease, his smooth touch left a warm trail everywhere but that one place where she desperately wanted it.

Fifi reached behind her and unclasped her bra, her ample breasts peeking out the sides as she held it in place, leaving him to beg for what she was hiding beneath. Suddenly shy, or so it seemed, she turned her head away and let go of the garment, earning a satisfied moan from the good doctor, feeling his firm ridge pulse between her legs, clearly pleased with the view.

Not one to turn down an invitation such as this, he grabbed her breasts firmly, stroking them, toying with them, kneading them until she moaned. Fifi leaned over him, brushing her rosy buds alongside his mouth, tempting him to take them. And he did.

Bain sat up, his hands cradling her ass, his head dipping down so his tongue could lash at her breasts. He stood, keeping her wrapped around his waist, and propped her against the wall with such grace and little effort. He knew what she wanted, and he was giving it to her like he'd done it a hundred times before.

When Fifi began to ride against him, he'd grind back, matching her pace and letting her lead. Bain let her sounds and movements decipher what she liked and what she wanted more of, letting her guide him as they explored each other's bodies with their needy hands and greedy mouths.

He pulled away only for a moment. "Are you sure?"

Fifi reached between them to undo his belt, nodding her head. "You have no idea."

Doc walked them down the hall to her bedroom and crawled on the bed, gently placing her in the middle. He hovered over her and undid her jeans before he sat back on his knees and dragged the rest of her clothing slowly down her legs. Completely bare, her legs still on either side of him, he stared with a clear view that left nothing to the imagination.

With pouty lips and heavy lids, Fifi arched slightly as her breaths became shallow. Having this man look at her this way was beyond sensual and just the other side of erotic. His blazing stare was nearly her undoing.

"So beautiful," he said.

A rush of bashfulness washed over her. Her knees came together, and she turned away, unable to control the fire he was stoking inside her.

"Fiona," he said. "Look at me, darlin'."

And she did.

There was something in his stare she couldn't explain. The heat of it was undeniable, emboldening her. She went out on a limb, feeling sexy…wanted…desired. She let her knees fall to the sides, exposing herself in the most vulnerable way, earning a guttural moan that could only be described as primal need. Doc took her invitation and stroked her, coaxing her, teasing her.

Bain pulled her to the edge of her bed and took to his knees so he could bury himself right where she wanted him. With each warm stroke of his tongue, her moans grew and her back arched. Sensing her near the finish, he stopped and stood, removing his pants so there was no longer a barrier between them.

Fifi scooted back on the bed, making room for him to join her. There was a slight pause from Doc, though, because there was no coming back from where they were about to go.

"Bain," she said, her voice a sultry moan.

That was all it took for him. He crawled onto the bed, placed himself between her legs, and that was where he stayed for the rest of the night.

7

Fifi woke in the warmth of summer rays peeking through the sheer curtains and the sound of birds chirping while a subtle breeze grazed her bare breasts — a simple reminder of the night before. Drifting in and out of a light slumber, she rolled to her side, arm extended. Her hand found the other side of the bed warm but empty.

A cold, wet nose nudged her forehead while the sound of purring interrupted by a cat's meow woke her completely.

"Missy?" Fifi said, scratching the cat's ears. "How'd you get in here? Bain said you didn't come in the house."

Then it hit her. *Bain*. She shot up only to grab her throbbing head while her stomach roiled.

"Oh my God. *Bain. Wine.* What have I done?" she said out loud, and the cat meowed in response.

A subtle throb between her legs reminded her exactly what she had done. For a moment, she was lost in the pleasant memory of how he made her body feel. Until reality set in, and she remembered she didn't do this. She didn't have one-night stands with handsome men — a man she didn't even like…or maybe she did?

"No. No. No," she said, shaking her aching head. "I told him I liked him. Why did I tell him that? I don't like him? Do I?"

The cat continued to dance around the bed, rubbing against Fifi's arm with the occasional meow as if responding to her every word.

"Oh, Missy." Fifi buried her head in her hands. "What have I done?"

Then what she had done came flooding back, and she realized just how naked she was when she'd done it.

"Oh no. Tell me I didn't…" She lifted the blanket, finding herself completely nude, and gasped. "Crap. I did. I showed him my… And touched his… We had…"

The cat became more aggressive, her meow more pronounced while she pitter-pattered at the blanket in Fifi's lap, the slight tapping of the cat's claws gaining Fifi's attention.

"What is it, Missy?" she asked, giving the animal her full attention and a pat. "Don't judge me. If you saw him without a shirt on, you'd take your clothes off too. What the hell am I saying? No. That can't happen again — no matter how… *good* he is at…*that*."

When the cat turned away and dug at the blanket next to Fifi a bit more aggressively than she had before, Fifi looked closer.

"What is it? You still smell him over there?" Fifi asked as the cat sat and began to gnaw. "I smell him too. Woodsy, masculine, a hint of citrus, and a lot of…*sexy*. Oh my God, Fifi. Stop."

She raked her hands through her hair, trying to decide what her next move would be. It was her house, so no walk of shame, but where had *he* gone? A subtle aroma began to fill the space. Coffee. He was still there.

More gnawing and now growling came from the cat when Fifi stroked her back.

"Seriously, Missy? Are you judging me or something? It's my bed. Get down." She shooed the animal.

When the cat obliged, it revealed the source of its distraction and left Fifi screaming. She jumped out of her bed and stood backed against the wall, dizzy from the sudden motion and remnants of too much wine the night before.

"Fiona?" Bain shouted, the sound of heavy feet running down the hallway. "Fiona, are you okay?"

Before she had a chance to react, he was in her doorway, bare chest, jeans hanging low on his narrow hips, a look of protective intensity that was as hot as it was intimidating on his face. Fifi would have liked to have blamed her current hangover for her delayed response and long stare, but it was simply the half-dressed man standing just feet away.

When his eyes raked over her, Fifi quickly remembered her state of dress, or lack thereof, and grabbed a blanket from the bed to cover herself.

"Seriously?" she spat. "A little privacy please. Have a little respect."

"You're kidding, right? I mean, I've already seen…*everything*. And you're the one screaming for help — I'm the *help* — so…how does that make me a bad guy?"

"Maybe it's the tongue hanging out and the drool, Bain. Jesus, you act like you've never seen a woman before."

"One, I've seen plenty of women." Bain paused, wishing he could take that back and rephrase it, given the look on Fifi's face. "Two, you said Jesus, and I thought you didn't like to borrow trouble."

With an exaggerated eye roll, she fired back, "Seriously? Just a regular…*playboy*, huh? A…*gigolo*? Such a lady's man, Doc."

"Certainly seemed like it was last night!" he defended. "You weren't complaining at alllll."

"How dare you. And I don't even remember last night, so it couldn't have been *that* good," Fifi lied. It *had been* that good. Just thinking about it made her core throb, nipples harden, and butterflies flutter in her belly.

"Looking a little flush there, Hollywood. Kind of like last night. Sure you don't remember?"

"Of course not. You know I had been drinking…I was clearly out of my mind drunk. What does that say about you?"

"Whoa. Don't go there. We were *both* feeling the alcohol, and we were both consenting. If I recall, it was *you* taking things to the next level, if you know what I mean."

He wasn't lying, and she regretted the not-so-subtle accusation she'd made. It was her who wanted it, pushed it, and dammit if she didn't want it now too, but you'd never get her to admit it.

"Well, like I said. Can't remember. Not a single thing. So don't flatter yourself, Doc. And for the record…*never again*!"

"That's what you say now, but we both know you're full of shit. That wasn't all alcohol talking, princess. And *for the record*, when you're ready for more…I'll remind you of this little chat." He waved his finger between them. "Now, what has you screaming? I mean…since it obviously wasn't me this time."

"You're disgusting," she fired back. "It's the cat. She put something on my bed, and I think she was…*eating it*."

"Missy? How'd she get in here?"

"Oh, I don't know. She wasn't feeling very chatty this morning." Fifi's words were dripping in sarcasm. "She was too busy killing things! Let me guess…a gift?"

Doc stepped over to the bed, pushed the blanket back, and laughed. "Wild jackrabbit. Those suckers are fast and hard to catch. She must really like you."

"Yeah, nothing says love like something *dead*."

"You're in her world now. She doesn't know any better, and after all this time, it says something if she still wants to impress you. Though, I can't think of a reason she would."

Fifi gasped in offense.

Doc grabbed a towel from the nearby laundry basket and wrapped up the dead rabbit. "I'll get it out of here and make sure the back door is closed. I'm guessing Nelson opened the sliding glass door again."

"The donkey? Are you serious? You really need to get this zoo under control. I can't be waking up to dead animals in my *bed*."

"Don't worry, Fiona. It'll all be over soon when you hop back into that heap of yours and head back to LA."

Doc Bain left the room, and Fifi felt his absence immediately. Lonely. Sad. She didn't know why she'd acted so harshly. It was just what came naturally. She didn't mean a word of what she'd said. The truth was, she remembered every detail from the previous night, and the majority of it was sans wine — all her. And if she really wanted to be honest, she was already craving more. She wanted to play doctor.

A knock on the door had Fifi rushing around to find something suitable to wear other than her birthday suit. It was, after all, past dawn and an acceptable time to go calling on neighbors...at least in McKenzie.

"Don't these people sleep?" she said to herself, tossing blankets as part of her search. "Where the hell is my suitcase?"

She settled for a pair of jean shorts and the only shirt she could find in a hurry. Doc's black T-shirt.

"You've got to be kidding me. I'm going to be swimming in this," she said to absolutely no one. "And no bra? Where did that thing go?"

On her way out of the room, she saw the plaid flannel he'd been wearing the night before and tossed it on, tying it at her waist. "There, that takes care of the loose boobs issue."

When the knocking persisted, she hollered, "I'm coming! I'm coming!"

She winced when she heard glass clatter from the kitchen and realized she wasn't alone, and her choice of words probably wasn't the greatest.

She palmed her forehead. "Get it together, Gallagher. He's just a man. A super good-looking and sexy with abs of steel — oh my God. Just stop. He's not your type and totally off-limits."

When the doorbell rang as she reached the front entrance, she whipped the door open, and said, "Some people actually sleep past the roosters! What do you want?"

Standing on her front stoop were more people than she cared to count at that hour without at least a cup or two of coffee in. The clipboards were a dead giveaway as to why they were there, and with Lou Shaw front and center, she knew she was in for it.

"Well, aren't you lookin' fancy." Lou snickered. "Rough night?"

Fifi ran her hands through her hair and tucked it behind her ears, then brushed them down her body as if it fixed the outfit by straightening it.

"Nope. I had a…fine night. What can I do for…all…of you?" she replied.

Lou marched past her, and the rest of the crowd followed.

Fifi opened the door wider and stepped aside, holding a hand out in welcome. "Please...come in."

"I already did," Lou said. "You sure you're feelin' all right, honey? Say, that's a familiar shirt."

"Yeah, I'm fine, and I...uh, found this shirt. Maybe someone left it behind after the party." *Nice save*, Fifi thought.

"Hmm. Perhaps," Lou said with a smarmy grin.

She *knew*. It was obvious, and all Fifi could do was shoot Lou a warning look not to say a thing because there was *nothing* to talk about — or nothing she was willing to talk about.

"Anyway. What's going on?" Fifi addressed the group she'd come to know as all the committee heads. "I didn't know there was some sort of festival or...committee meeting this morning?"

"Oh, there wasn't. Just an emergency came up, and since no one was privy to Dee's plan, you're our go to," Lou said.

"Oh. Okay. An emergency. Seems urgent then," Fifi stuttered, not knowing the first thing about planning a Christmas festival...in the middle of July. "I wasn't privy to her plan either, but let's see if we can figure this stuff out."

"Now, I'm just here as a mediator," Lou went on. "I'm sort of the head of all the committees, so when there's a problem, I solve it. This one here, however, lands on your turf, honey."

"Turf? Seriously?" Fifi snickered, thinking back to her previous thought of small-town mafia when she'd arrived. When nobody joined her with so much as a giggle, her expression became serious. "Okay. So, uh...what seems to be the problem?"

The crowd all began to talk at once. When talking turned to harsh tones and near yelling to full-blown arguing, Fifi put her two fingers in her mouth and blew the highest-pitch whistle she could muster.

"Well, I'll be damned." Lou snorted. "You do have a bit of Dee in ya, honey. Well, go on. The floor's yours. You got their attention."

"It's too early for this level of crazy, and none of this is serious enough to fight over," Fifi scolded. "Now, let's all remember our manners and take turns, m'kay?"

Lou smiled with pride and tossed Fifi an approving wink.

Each of them took turns telling their tales of woe and why their issue was more pressing than the others. Everything from fighting with the Fourth of July committee, who refused to accompany them, to damaged decorations left by the tragic fires, and even a candy cane shortage was tossed on the table to discuss.

"Okay, give me a minute on the damaged decorations. I need to wrap my mind around that to come up with a solution. And no lights on the live trees due to wildfire season," she said, going down the mental list she'd made. "I think I have a few ideas for that too. I agree replacing the decorations this time of year will be costly, but surely, candy canes can't be that expensive. Give me a second."

Fifi pulled out her phone and began to scroll through a search for candy canes.

"Aha!" Fifi said, jumping in excitement. "Mission accomplished. Candy canes sourced! Best part, they're just one town over…which is odd they have that many candy canes at the general store, but…"

"Whoa," one of the members said. "You don't mean the Arrow Springs General Store, do you?"

A round of gasps and sighs followed.

"Um, yes?" Fifi answered.

"Oh no, that won't do. That won't do at all," another

member said. "They must know. Oh dear…we have a leak. Or a mole."

Fifi listened around the room as it went up in a frenzy over *candy canes.*

"Does someone want to fill me in here? What's the big deal? They're just candy canes. And, like, twenty minutes away…please tell me the problem with that," Fifi said, tossing her hands in the air.

"Well, they clearly bought out everything they could," Lou clarified. "They're a bunch of dirty bastards over there, taking advantage of our town tragedy like that."

"I still don't understand," Fifi questioned. "Why would it matter where you buy them?"

"So, we have to come crawlin' to them for help and pay a small fortune. We beat them every year in the *Destination Magazine's* 'most desirable vacation location.' It turns out, they're a little pissed off about it because they have a carousel in their town center and we don't."

"Again, what does that have to do with candy canes?" Fifi asked, clearly irritated.

"It's obvious," Lou said, not sure why Fifi wasn't catching on. "They hijacked all the candy canes they could so we'd have no choice but to come groveling to them and asking to buy their candy canes at a premium. Oooh, they'd love to see us on our hands and knees like that."

"You can't be serious." Fifi looked around the room. "That sounds pretty petty for an entire town to get behind. I mean, they aren't the *only* candy canes out there, just the closest. The world's a pretty big place."

Lou pointed at Fifi's phone. "Look there on that Google box of yours again. Tell me where you see more candy canes."

"Okay." Fifi nodded with confidence and began to scroll through her phone. "Ha. Found some."

"Uh-huh," Lou said, wearing a knowing grin.

"And…oh…" Fifi said, reading the fine print.

Lou chuckled. "China?"

"Yep. They're all coming from China and take weeks to get here." Fifi shook her head and tucked her phone in her pocket. "How is it you can't get a candy cane anywhere…in July?"

"Because they're all in China," Lou said, "Or Arrow Springs…"

"Okay, so we go to the store manager—" Fifi began.

Lou interrupted. "Who also happens to be the town mayor, but go on…"

"Okay, we go to the mayor slash manager of the store and tell him what's going on. Surely he's aware of what happened last year. Maybe he'll be sympathetic and do the neighborly thing and cut us a deal?"

"Ha!" Lou said. "Why do you think Dee had a code in that calendar you found?"

Fifi shrugged.

"For this very reason. They copy us every single year trying to top us and make number one in *Destination Magazine*. They've played some dirty tricks, stolen decorations, intercepted our Santa one year, and even took the baby Jesus's manger and Nelson from our live nativity. I'm surprised they haven't burned their town to the ground just so they could have their Christmas in July too. Dirty, dirty, dirty. Bunch of old fogies runnin' stuff over there."

The crowd began to chat amongst themselves, discussing all the dirty deeds of the Arrow Springs committee over the years.

"Okay. Okay." Fifi ran her hands through her hair. "Meet

me in the town center at noon, and I'll have a plan. Meanwhile, stop talking to the Fourth of July festival committee. Sounds like you're pissing them off, and we may need them."

Lou smiled as she forced everyone out the door. Before she closed it behind her, she stopped and said to Fifi, "Now there's the girl I knew was in there. Just like your grandmother."

And she left.

Fifi fell back on the couch and closed her eyes. She really had her work cut out for her with this festival and not a single clue as to where she should start.

"All right, Gram," Fifi said to herself. "You got my attention. Where do I begin?"

8

"We ain't budging one bit, Gallagher. I know those fuss buckets were over at your place bright and early," a man Fifi didn't recognize said as he approached her. "The decorations always go up a week before the Fourth of July festival and stay up the week of. We already made a compromise to let them come in July fifth and redecorate for the Christmas festival. It's important to the town that we celebrate Christmas, so it's important to us, but that's as far as we go."

When the man reached her, Fifi could smell a familiar aroma. It was sweet, yeasty, and felt like home.

She smiled at the man. "Jed? Jed Baker?"

The man's furrowed brow and stiff stance softened. "Why, yes. So, you *do* remember me."

"Of course I do! The first thing I did every summer was stop at the bakery for your famous apple fritters and maple bars," Fifi admitted, throwing her arms around the man. "In fact, I already had my first fritter and didn't even have to come to town for it."

Jed Baker owned Baker's Bakery, a significant landmark in McKenzie Ridge as it had been made nearly famous by multiple Food Network shows that had featured his bakery. Fifi wasn't sure why her initial instinct was to hug the man, but then she hadn't been sure about much since returning to McKenzie. It had only been a handful of days, and this place was changing her. And she didn't hate it.

"I'm sorry we couldn't make it your grandmother's going away party," Jed said, full of sympathy. "We were already committed to a wedding in Portland. You might remember those O'Reilly kids from the summers you were here. Well, my boy married one of them, and they seem to be marrying off one after the other."

"I do remember them. The boys were always in trouble." She laughed. "I assume it was Carrigan O'Reilly BJ married? I had a feeling with those two."

"I think everyone did but them." Jed laughed. "So, what can I do to help you, Fifi? I'll do anything I can to help make this a success…in your grandmother's honor, of course."

And that's how you win over the opposition, Fifi thought.

"I may have a solution to satisfy everyone. Ever seen a red, white, and blue Christmas?"

Promptly at noon, the rest of the committee heads showed up at town center, where Fifi was already laying out a plan. With limited time and resources, she came up with an epic event like nothing McKenzie had seen before…mostly because Christmas in July wasn't a thing, but that was just being technical.

"Here's the idea." She started. "We are going to run with the red, white, and blue theme for Christmas week. We'll hang theme-colored lights on all the noninflammable décor, as per the fire marshal. There are plenty of white ornaments, but nothing else made it, so…spray paint and hang them during the Fourth of July festival. The fourth cookie committee has agreed to change out the red, white, and blue cookies to — drum roll please — red, white, and blue candy cane cookies. Arrow Springs can suck on all those candy canes they hijacked for all I care."

"Well, what about the cocoa?" a woman asked. "We always put the candy canes in the cocoa."

"Turns out there's a cocoa shortage this time of year, and I have no clue what my grandmother ordered or didn't order. If it shows up, we'll just be ahead for December. Since it's really flippin' hot and only getting hotter, we're opting for lemonade stations in lieu of cocoa stations. Optional strawberries and blueberries to keep up with our color scheme. You guys with me? Because I'm just getting started."

"This doesn't sound very traditional," someone said.

"Neither is Christmas…in *July*. I think we're good," Fifi argued, standing her ground. "We'll bring in as many traditional elements as we can and give them a summer flair so they make sense for the season. All the important things will be there."

"I couldn't agree more," Granny Lou said. "You're off to a good start, missy. What else ya got?"

"Meet me here tomorrow. Let's make it noon again. I'll have a more detailed plan, and we can start delegating."

"Tomorrow at noon?" a man said from the crowd. "I thought we had a meeting at the Ponderosa to…*discuss some things*?"

"Hey, I was supposed to meet you at the Ponderosa," another man said.

When the light chatter turned to a roar, Fifi did that high-pitched whistle again. "Yeah, yeah…I set you guys up. I was meeting all of you at the same time — there, now you know. Let's just get this out of the way now since we're all together. I'm not a referee. You're all adults, so work out your problems. And remember why we're all here, to begin with. It's for the town, so get over it and get along."

With that, Fifi turned on her heels and headed for her car to the sound of Lou cheering her on in the background and the bantering crowd silent. Mission accomplished.

"Mission accomplished...*for now*," Fifi said to herself. "Maybe Lou's right, and I am more like you than I thought, Gram."

* * *

FIFI FELT EMPOWERED AND MORE CONFIDENT THAN THE DAY she'd arrived. She was cruising down the road with the windows down and Christmas music blaring for inspiration as she planned the best red, white, and blue Christmas shindig she could possibly imagine.

McKenzie Ridge wasn't her endgame, but she didn't hate being there anymore and actually looked forward to the coming weeks. Being in town, even for a short spell, brought back so many warm memories, as did the kind faces she'd reacquainted with. McKenzie would be a nice break from the real world, and she'd have plenty of downtime to put her pen to paper and finally finish the manuscript she'd spent far too long on already.

"If only McKenzie were closer to LA," Fifi said out loud, slapping her steering wheel to the beat of the music. "I could keep Gram's place and use it for a weekend getaway or summer spot where I come to write."

She pondered that idea, trying to gain more pros than cons to keeping the home and having a secret getaway spot that gave her all the feels. The cons far outweighed the pros, simply by logistics and the daunting workload that would always be waiting for her in Los Angeles. Something about that thought weighed heavily on her, dampening her carefree mood.

"Doc could stay, and his animals would still have a home," she thought out loud, giving Doc Bain credit in the pro column. "I mean, at least it isn't like the place would be empty. And since it's paid for, the rent he pays could cover the expenses that naturally come with a property like that. Who am I kidding? How often would I really make it back here? The only reason I'm here now is because I have to be, and in the grand scheme of things, it's just making the work back home stack up. Hugging the donut man must've messed with my head. This is a bad idea," she concluded.

From the corner of her eye, Fifi saw movement on the right side of the road. It was headed her way, right in front of her fast-moving car. She swerved to miss whatever it was but overcorrected when her tires got caught on loose gravel, throwing her left, then right again, and into the ditch off the shoulder where her car stopped with a thud and died.

Fifi sat still for a moment as she caught her breath, trying to decide if everything was fine or everything hurt, but she couldn't tell. Climbing out the driver's side window, she held her phone in the air, attempting to catch a signal so she could call for help. No signal. Of course.

"Crap!" she yelled. "This is why it would never work here. They don't even have decent cell service."

She turned to look at her car, the nose buried in the loose clay, the backend in the air, tires still slowly spinning. As if on cue, there was a loud pop and steam began to rise from under the creased hood.

"Of course." She tossed her hands in the air. "That's all I need — to start a forest fire while I'm out here and land myself in prison for arson."

She popped the trunk and pulled out a couple of bottled

waters she kept stowed there for emergencies. She always thought an emergency would be stuck on the 101 freeway — or worse — I-405 in hundred-degree temperatures during, say…an earthquake. It turned out, her emergency was a lonely mountain road in the middle of nowhere with no cell service, surrounded by wild beasts, and a smoking car mere feet from a dry, combustible forest.

"Yep. This place isn't for me," she said before looking up and yelling to no one in particular, "C'mon! I can't die out here like this. It's…*hot*. And…bears."

She sat for a moment, contemplating whether she should continue east toward home — her grandmother's home, rather — or west back to town. Either way, she had a good mile or two of walking, and the flip-flops she had on weren't going to be very kind.

A low roar caught her attention and suddenly became a cloud of dust in the distance, growing in size as it came her way.

She looked back at the sky. "Help. That didn't take long. Thank you, universe. I wasn't meant to die out here. Not in this outfit, anyway."

It was a truck. She could see it now through the plume of dirt still camouflaging her knight, or dame, in shining armor.

When the truck came to a halt, she ran to the passenger side window and leaned in. "Hey, don't suppose you have a phone that works out here? Or—"

She paused, realizing just who the universe sent her way. "Crap, it's you."

"You know, I could just keep on goin' down this road, and you can wait for the next guy, which will be me again because I'm the only one who travels this road given the only place it leads is the farm." Bain winked. "But I get it. You'd rather wait."

Doc put the truck in gear and inched forward when she hollered for him to stop. "Okay. I get it. I need…you. I mean, I need your help," she quickly corrected, leaving the potentially misinterpreted innuendo off the table.

"Hop in. I'm headed to town now," Bain said.

"Oh, good. I need a craft store." Fifi said. "I need to get supplies for my vision board."

"Your…what?"

"Vision board. I will put everything for the festival on it so it's easy for everyone to…*envision* too." Fifi went on. "It's to keep everyone on track and help motivate people too."

"Okay. A vision board it is…sounds *perfect*. We can stop at Reggie's garage and tell him where we left your car," Bain said. "He'll get it out of the ditch and let you know what it needs…since it's steaming."

"You want me to just…leave it here? Unattended?"

"Since it's illegal for squirrels to drive, I'm pretty sure it'll be safe."

"Oh, I'm not so sure about that. It was one of your little furry friends that caused this to begin with. For all I know, it was so he could steal my car. I'd believe anything at this point." Fifi leaned into her car and pulled out her purse before turning back to Doc, who reached across the truck and opened the door for her to climb in. "It literally sat on the side of the road and waited for me. I saw it!"

"That must've been Roger."

"Oh, you have got to be kidding me. He's one of yours?"

"No. I just call them all Roger because they look the same. They like to play chicken."

"It's on purpose?" Fifi asked.

"I doubt it, but who really knows. Animals can have quirky personalities. Maybe they run because they get nervous, or maybe it's to screw with people. Who really knows?" Doc said, continuing down the road toward town.

"Wait. Aren't you going to turn around?" Fifi asked.

"No, why would I do that? I said we'd head to town."

"I just came from there," Fifi reasoned.

"You said you needed a craft store, so…"

"Right," she said. "I do. But I was headed home to change really quick. I left the house sans hair and makeup and thought I'd get that taken care of before I headed in to shop."

"Let me get this straight. You were already in town, as is. No hair and makeup, whatever that means. But you were going to go home just to brush your hair and go right back to town?" Bain was confused, but then Fifi tended to cause that…often.

"Yes. I had no choice. I had until noon and wasn't really planning on seeing anyone who hadn't already seen me in a less than presentable state. Now that I'm facing the rest of the public, I should probably look my best, first impressions and all."

Doc scratched his head. "That's the craziest thing I think you've said so far. It doesn't make any sense. I'm pretty sure nobody in town cares if you're wearing lipstick or not. It isn't front-page news. Who're you trying to impress, anyway? People in this town already know you, or at least feel like they do, thanks to Dee. So, I'd say it's high time you…*get over yourself.*"

Fifi gasped. "Well, someone woke up on the wrong side of the bed this morning."

"Actually, I was mighty fine on my side of the bed this morning. Smile on my face and everything. It's what happened after that *pissed* me off."

"*I* pissed *you* off?"

"Seems you found your stick and firmly placed it right back up your—"

"Whoa. Is that going to be your go-to jab? It's juvenile and beneath you, *Doctor*."

"And you'd know about things beneath me, so…"

"You're disgusting," she fired back.

"And you're a pain in the ass, *Hollywood*."

Fifi squinted her eyes, giving Bain a sharp glare. "You have no idea. By the way, your truck smells like manure."

"Manure? Darlin', I think that's your attitude you're smelling." Doc winked.

9

"Doc?" Fifi hollered in a panic through the barn. "Doc! I need help. You in here?"

Doc casually popped out of one of the stalls, drying his hands on a towel, to find Fifi holding her sloth on one hip with a large bulletin-type board under the other arm.

"We weren't supposed to head to town for another hour so…"

"I…uh, need help. I'm really worried about Dallas." Fifi propped her board against the wall and quickly made her way to Doc, handing over Dallas. "Something's wrong with him."

Sensing her emotion, he quickly changed his demeanor and took the animal from her, moving to an exam room, and began to look over the animal. "What's going on with him?"

"I-I don't know. He just isn't being himself. I can tell… something is wrong." Fifi went on.

"Okay. Can you tell me what that means? What is he doing out of the ordinary?"

"Well, for starters, he's lethargic."

Doc paused and gave Fifi a serious look. "Uh, he's a sloth."

"I know," she fussed. "More so than usual. He isn't usually this…slow or tired."

"I want to believe you, but sloths all have one speed, and it's barely there. They also sleep like twenty hours a day, so maybe he's napping," Doc reasoned. "Anything else that can help me out here?"

"Um…he isn't really eating. Or drinking. He hasn't been playing."

"He…plays? Really?"

"Well, I play with the feather on a stick or the ball, but he watches. It's kind of like playing, and he wouldn't look at me this morning with the feather."

"You play…with cat toys…to entertain your…*sloth*?" Bain pushed down the laughter that was threatening.

"Yes. Yes, I do. Are you making fun of me? They encourage it at play group."

"You take your sloth to a play group?" Now, the laughter was out in the world because Doc just couldn't help himself. "Something tells me there are more domestic sloths in LA than their natural habitat in the rain forest."

"Yes. It's a thing back home, and there's a good-size population of sloth as pets. It's like going to the gym or a mommy and me thing but with your pet. We go to sloth Sunday. He loves it."

"I doubt he even knows he's there, but okay." Bain snorted. "What's he been eating?"

"His usual. Fruits, leafy greens, dried meal worms. Sometimes he sneaks things he's not supposed to, though," she said.

"And how would he do this sneaking thing given the lack of pace he has? Sloth and sneaky aren't typically used together."

"Believe me. He can move if he wants to. Sometimes, if

I'm distracted or, like, in the shower, he'll swipe something if I accidentally leave it within reach."

"Okay, I suppose that makes sense. Has he swiped anything that you know of?"

"No, but with all those people at the house for Gram's memorial, there's a good chance he got something. Please, I know I'm not your favorite person, but he is all I have left. He can't be sick. He needs to be okay."

Bain sensed her desperation and felt badly for giving her a hard time. "Okay. When is the last time he…you know… went to the bathroom?"

"Well, not since we've been here." Fifi shrugged

"It can be a couple of weeks between, you know, bowel movements, in these guys. I can keep him here and observe him. I have a tech on when I'm not. We can figure it out."

"Really? You'd do that for me?"

"Yeah…I would," Bain said, locked in her gaze. He shook his head and came to his senses. "But mostly for him."

"Of course," Fifi said. "For Dallas. I get it. Because you and animals…"

"We sort of have a thing," Bain said.

"Do you now?" She snickered.

"Not that kind of thing. Are you going to ruin everything? Like every moment, just…squash it? I mean a connection."

"Right" – Fiona nodded with a smirk – "like Dr. Doolittle."

"Exact—" Bain shook his head. "You know, I can tell you right now something is going on with Dallas we can address right away."

Fifi matched Bain's sudden serious demeanor. "Oh really? So, something is wrong? What is it?"

"He's depressed," Bain said. "Struggling a bit with anger."

"Oh my God. That sounds serious. Is it because of the new environment? They can be so sensitive."

"Yeah, maybe a little bit of the environment. But mostly, it's the clothes you put on him."

"Are you an animal behaviorist? How did you get all of that out of a quick visit?"

"No, not at all. It's because I'm a guy, and if someone dressed me in pink sweaters, tutus, and hair bows, I'd be pissed and probably depressed too." Bain shrugged.

"Wow. Classy." Fifi glared. "For the record, he needs warm, humid environments. So…sweaters."

"They have to be pink? And the bows don't offer humidity, nor do the tutus."

"No, they're just cute! He doesn't care what he wears! He's a *sloth*."

"Are you sure about that? I mean…I *am* the expert," Bain said. "I think we're due in town. Let's head out."

"How about I just go by myself? There's an extra truck around here. Let me see the keys."

Bain tossed said keys in the air and caught them. "Not a chance. Last I checked, you liked to park in ditches, and I think you're too short to see over the hood of that truck. I'll drive ya."

"Can we at least take the one that *doesn't* smell like your job?"

Doc sucked his teeth, making a high-pitched sound. "Sorry, gotta see a guy about a horse. Manure truck it is."

"Of course it is," she said. "Since you brought it up…I know you have always served as co-chair on the Christmas festival committee."

"I didn't bring that up. I never said a word about that," Bain replied.

"Yeah, I know…so I guess I'm bringing it up. FYI, it's a

two-person job, so the whole town will be counting on your help this year as the person who worked closest to my gram. We all really...*need* you."

"You really do play dirty, Gallagher. And for the record, I was just Dee's sounding board and occasional driver."

"So, what I'm hearing is, you won't mind being my driver or sounding board." Fifi smiled as she climbed into the truck. "Like I said, don't want to let the *whole* town down."

"Hmph. Guess you're right," Bain said as he rolled up the windows. "Looks like we'll be spending a lot of time together...in *this* truck."

"Wait. Why are you rolling up the windows? It...smells, and it's like eighty degrees outside."

"Yep, sure is. But see, I have allergies, and, uh...the window down just makes them a bit worse." He cleared his throat. "Windows up, darlin'."

"Okay, can you please turn on the a/c? That ought to help with the smell...and heat."

"Dang thing's busted. Can you believe it? *Darn.*"

"Who's playing dirty now, Doc?"

"Why...I don't know what you're talking about." Bain smiled, pleased with the victory.

* * *

"Now that your *vision board* is in the Grange Hall for all the committees and volunteers to refer to, what's left to do?" Bain asked.

"Oh, that's all I needed. I just wanted to make sure it was here before we *really* kicked things off," Fifi said. "Is it just me, or did they seem a little...*not excited* about the vision board? I mean, it was a good idea, right? It makes sense?"

Doc snickered. "I'm sure they'll come to appreciate it. Folks just do things differently around here, that's all."

"It's…organized," Fifi defended. "If they have any questions or want to know how something should look—"

"Vision board. I get it," he interrupted. "Now, you still haven't answered my question. Is there anything else you need to do while we're in town?"

"No…just that. With the Fourth of July festival kicking off tonight, there isn't much we *can* do other than wait out the week until we can start decorating for Christmas."

"Good. Then come with me." Doc nodded toward the town center, indicating for her to follow. "Tonight is the artist spotlight. All kinds of cool stuff to see."

"Are you asking me on a date, Jensen Bain?"

"Uh. No. As co-chairperson, I thought it might be a good idea for you to wander a bit, see what the fourth committee tossed together. You know…research. Find…inspiration for your vision board. And let's drop the first name. It's not as endearing as you think."

"Oh. Well. I suppose a little inspiration doesn't hurt anyone. Lead the way."

"Will do. I think some of these locals might impress you with their talents."

"Oh, I don't know. I've worked with some of the best in the industry…it takes a lot to impress me. I'm used to six-to-seven-figure budgets, and that's just for set design."

"I've seen some stuff made of pinecones and wax that will blow your mind."

"Pinecones...*really*?"

"Oh yeah. Antlers too. Now that's some really cool stuff."

"Lead the way…"

Doc wasn't wrong. Fifi was impressed all right. So much so, she started taking pictures and jotting down notes in her phone. They went from booth to booth, each one earning an *ooh* or an *aah*. Her most treasured find was the farmers' stands with all of their fresh fruit and vegetables.

"Are you about done here?" Doc asked, arms full of produce and knickknacks she'd collected throughout the afternoon. "I'm about out of arm space to carry anything more."

"Oh, you'll manage." She chuckled. "There are only two more booths, and we are just in time for the live music to start in Pavilion Park."

"I thought this wasn't a date," Doc teased.

"Don't get your hopes up. It isn't." Fifi smiled. "It's research and inspiration, remember?"

"And live music will inspire…"

"Well, we want to make sure the carolers and such are up to speed. Back-to-back events like this mean these guys are setting the standard."

"Good point," Doc said. "So, you planning on making a stew or cobbler with all these fruits and vegetables or something?"

"Me? Cook? No…that wouldn't be a good idea. I love food, terrible at making it," Fifi joked. "I thought Nelson might like the carrots. I was picking them out of my salad yesterday, and he devoured them. The popcorn's for Timber — who knew turkeys liked popcorn? I was sitting outside writing last night and popped a bag. Timber kept stealing it, so I thought a bag that size might last him."

"You…got it for the animals?"

"Yeah. I can't think of anything for Maude, though. And I think she already hates me, so maybe I should grab some fancy cat food for her or something? I think she peed on my flip-flops on the deck. The rest is for Ben and the other animals. I read that buffalo like berries and, like…lettuce. I just want to be fair."

Doc was impressed by her efforts. She was falling for the animals, which wasn't hard. But he hoped it would be enough to maybe make her fall for McKenzie and stick around.

"So, uh, what about Missy? I mean, dead bird and rabbit…the cat's a serial killer. Seems like she's the one you want to piss off the least."

"Oh, I already figured her out." Fifi snickered. "I also figured out why Gram had so many cans of tuna in the pantry. We're on good terms now. You know, I think you were right, she just missed me and wanted me to notice her. Imagine, after all those years, she remembered me?"

"I can't imagine ever forgetting someone like you," Doc said sweetly. Even he was surprised he'd said it out loud and quickly recovered when he heard her soft gasp. "I mean, you sort of cause a scene and stuff."

"Oh. Is that right?" There was disappointment in her tone despite trying to cover it up. "Well, it's still…*sweet.*"

Now it was unclear if she was still talking about the cat or Doc's subliminal slip. Either way, it was clear he struck a nerve and hurt her feelings, which had never been his intention. Spending the afternoon with her, no heated arguments or negative banter, was wearing on him. She was wearing on him. And if he were willing to face the truth, he'd see his feelings for her started when she jumped behind him to hide from the buffalo her first day in McKenzie.

Sure, it helped that he already knew something about her from all of Dee's stories, but there was just something about her presence. The whole town was starting to fall for her too. At each booth they'd stopped at, she'd made a new friend or caught up with an old one. As they moved from booth to booth, she managed to get people on her team, willing to support the Christmas festival in one way or another with their skills and wares.

There was something magical about her. Doc was sure she'd sparkle if the sun hit her just right because she was just that special. There was no sense in clinging to false hopes or a silly adoration. She was leaving and all the reasons he thought she was great were all the reasons she belonged in LA — not McKenzie.

"Why is everyone looking at us weird?" Doc asked, burying his thoughts.

"Us?" Fifi asked.

"Don't you see it?" he asked.

"Oh, they're probably just looking at me because I'm so beautiful. People, especially women, are really intimidated by my beauty sometimes," Fifi said with confidence. "It's hard to be pretty."

Doc stopped in his tracks, suddenly recanting the idea of special and magical where she was concerned. "Are you…are you…serious right now? I mean, you're beautiful, but do you really…*think that*?"

"I mean…" She shrugged. "Or it could be because your fly is down."

"My fly? Why didn't you tell me?" Doc quickly dropped the goods he'd been carrying around and fixed his fly.

"Who's causing a scene now, Doc?" She laughed, walking off without him.

"Turns out, you're kind of an ass," Bain fired back.

"Takes one to know one!" she hollered over her shoulder, still laughing.

"Real mature, *Fiona*."

10

The week went by in a total blur. While the Fourth of July festival was in full force, Fifi and all her committees were behind the scenes creating Christmas magic. As pieces of the Fourth of July festivities were no longer needed, they were converted to Christmas and staged by Fifi's team of help. They'd even taken the Fourth of July floats and converted them to Christmas floats, literally as they finished the parade route. There wasn't a moment to spare, and Fifi was in her element. This was what she did best: take one set and make it look like something from another world.

Despite limited notice, she was able to secure her version of Christmas — and on a tight budget…of nearly zero.

"I can't believe you've pulled so much together," Doc said. "The trees you had the kids from art camp paint are brilliant. Honestly, I don't know what you need me for. I don't know how, but you've made Christmas in July…*normal.*"

She patted his shoulder. "You're my driver. And my muscle. Can you move these six-footers over to the wall so they can finish drying? And Christmas in July *is* normal…it's McKenzie."

"Touché. Speaking of driving," Doc said, moving the oversized wooden tree cutout painted by the Art on the Prairie camp kids. "Reggie said your car should be done in about a week. He finally found the last part, and it should be here Monday so you can be on the road…you know…"

Fifi paused. "When the festival is over?"

"Yeah," Doc said. "How's that for timing?"

"Yeah…" She forced a smile and faux giggle. Truth be told, she was just getting used to the place and was hoping he'd need a few more weeks.

"That doesn't sound very convincing. I thought you were ready to get back to La-La Land."

"Oh, I am. I just…" She couldn't say it. Why put it in the universe if it wasn't a possibility? So, she faked it, like every girl had at least once in her life. "I…uh, just thought a few extra days to finish up my manuscript would be good. I've written more in the short time I've been in town than I have in the past eighteen months."

"Maybe stay then. I mean…if you're close to finishing. You don't have the house ready to list anyway."

He wasn't wrong. She hadn't done a single thing to prep the house for sale. She'd spent every free moment writing and putting the festival together.

"I'll probably just have to hire a moving company or something. Let them pack it all up and put it in storage, and I'll go through it when I have a chance."

"Makes sense. Or I could help you if you want to sort stuff first?"

"Oh, no. We tried that once. Didn't end well."

"If I recall, it did end well. You just didn't want to admit it the next morning."

"Yeah, let's not go there. I kind of don't find you insanely annoying at the moment…so don't ruin it," she teased as Doc walked off to take a call.

Fifi and Doc had been spending a lot of time together over the past several days. Their once low-blow jabs had become innocent, friendly teasing. She kept him company in the barn while he was treating patients, and she was visiting Dallas, who was still under observation. Doc had brought in an old log, stripped off its bark, and gave it a place in the barn for Dallas to feel more at home. They'd come a long way in a few short weeks.

"Hey, I have to head out. Got an emergency call. I can come back for ya, but it might be a little later, or I can have Lou drive ya?"

"Emergency?" An odd tone in Doc's voice had her on alert. She looked around the room and saw a to-do list a mile long, but there was a subtle lingering nudge to step outside her comfort zone.

"Hey, Lou. Doc and I have to head out. You got this?" Fifi asked.

"Honey…do *I* got this? Does a squirrel's nuts sweat in summer?"

"Um, I wouldn't know, nor do I want to. You've got my cell number if you need me for anything."

Lou winked. "You betcha."

"Let's go, Bain."

As they walked out the door and jumped in the truck, Bain stopped. "You know you don't *have* to go right now. I wouldn't leave you stranded."

"I know. The idea of riding home with Lou had me a little…cringy. I'm pretty sure she has half the town's single men lined up to dance with me next week. Something tells me she'd take the long way home just to fill me in on all of them — down to height, income, and fertile years left."

"And by long way, you mean through Canada." Bain laughed.

"I see you've had the same car ride. Did you know she packs a pistol *and* a flask in that big purse of hers?"

Doc snorted. "Everyone knows. Blake — you know, local police? He keeps confiscating the thing and she keeps finding it and taking it back. Nobody knows how she does it. So now, he just takes her bullets. She has no idea it isn't loaded."

"I love that. As quirky as it is, it's sweet. You wouldn't hear of a thing like that in LA. If an old lady has a weapon, it's because she's using it." She giggled. "Good luck getting those bullets."

"Definitely keeps things interesting around here," he said as they made their way out of town.

"You know, you're right. There is *always* something going on around here. It's kind of fun. I didn't expect that."

"What did you expect?" Bain asked, genuinely interested.

"I don't know, really. I guess I thought the childhood memories I had were just that…childlike. Everything is fun at grandma's when you're a kid, right? But McKenzie is exactly as I remember it." She shrugged. "It's fun. So tell me, what's this emergency we're headed to? Porcupine in labor? Bullfrog with a broken leg?"

"Not exactly, though both of those would be interesting to treat. Dawson Taylor just got hit by a deer on the backroads."

"You mean he hit a deer?" Fifi corrected.

"No, it hit him," Bain said. "Happens a lot more than you'd think."

"Oh no. How bad is it?"

"That's the thing, he doesn't know. Can't find it."

"Then it might be okay. That's a good thing."

Bain shook his head. "It's a small one, left a good-sized dent in the door of his truck."

"So you're going to go find it?" Fifi questioned.

"No. *We're* going to go find it. At least try. If it was small like he said, and all alone…we may be looking at an orphan. Even if it's fine, it doesn't stand a chance on its own."

"A baby." Sadness filed Fifi's tone. "We'll find it."

Bain looked at her, amused, or maybe he was slightly impressed by her reaction — perhaps both. She was already watching out her window, looking through the woods despite being a handful of miles away from the scene.

This place really was wearing on her. *Interesting*, he thought.

"That must be them," Fifi said, pointing ahead.

"Yep. That's Dawson's truck." Bain confirmed. "And that little girl with the sad face is his daughter."

"Oh no. She saw it happen!" Fifi said. "That must've scared her."

Doc pulled up behind Dawson's truck and got out to meet them. "So, we think it's a small one?"

"I could hardly tell, it happened so fast. It hit the rear door, driver side," Dawson said, leading them to the truck. "I probably wouldn't have stopped after it took off like that, but El insisted. She saw it run, so…"

He extended his hand to Fifi. "Hi there. You must be Fiona Gallagher. Dawson Taylor, and this is my daughter, Ellie."

"You can call me Fifi. I've heard the name. You're one of the festival volunteers. Nice to finally have a face to go with it," Fifi said, then turned her attention to Ellie. "That must've frightened you. I'm very sorry that happened."

"Nah, I'm not scared. I'm just worried cuz it's just an itty-bitty baby, and it's all alone with no mama. We gotta find it. Right, Miss Fifi?"

Fifi looked at the two men standing side by side, grinning

at the little girl, and had no doubt the big weepy doe eyes looking back at them were going to get exactly that — a hunt for the baby deer.

"Did you see the dent in my daddy's truck?" the little girl asked. "I'm sure he has a bad headache, and he's hurt super bad."

When Fifi took in the dent the girl pointed out, she noticed a smudge of what appeared to be blood, and her heart sank.

"Oh no. It *is* hurt, isn't it?" She looked at the men, who both shrugged. "Yes, Ellie. We're going to find it, and Doc's going to help it. Don't you worry. Want to be a team and search together?"

Doc reached out to grab Fifi's arm as she and the girl walked by, and whispered, "Hey, don't make promises you can't keep to that kiddo. *If* we find it, there's no telling what condition it's going to be in."

"It'll be fine. And you can fix it if it isn't," Fifi whispered back.

"Fiona, it doesn't work that way," Doc said, his tone turned serious. "If we find it alive, we still may not be able to save it. I might have to put it down if it's hurt too bad."

Fifi gasped. "You'll do no such thing. I have faith in you, Doctor. We *will* find it, and you *will* help it. Everything is going to be okay…just ask that sweet little girl."

Doc shook his head while extending his pointed hand toward the woods on the other side of the vehicles. "Be my guest. Walk straight in so it's easy to turn around and find your way out. Spread out several feet, but close enough that you can quickly reach each other. Dawson and I will flank either side of you so you and Ellie are sandwiched in and don't get lost."

"Look who's bossy now," Fifi teased. "Let's find a baby deer."

Fifi marched into the woods, holding Ellie's hand at first, then branching out so they were a handful of feet apart. The group walked slow and quiet, trying to find their patient. The farther in they went, the quieter it got as the animals sensed a predator…from LA.

It was almost eerie, only hearing your own footsteps against breaking branches on the forest floor and the sound of your own heartbeat whooshing with a melodic thump, forcing you to march with the beat. Fifi had never experienced such quiet; it was almost lonely and frightening.

But the very things that made it uneasy and a little hair-raising were what clued Fifi in. When the sound of the ground shifting off-beat stood out, her senses heightened. She heard subtle movement, maybe a sweeping of the brush or kick of a pinecone. Even the pine needles covering the ground created a small sound only small feet could kick up — and it wasn't from them.

Fifi stopped and looked around. There was movement in the brush, but she couldn't see anything out of the ordinary. She moved in slowly, quietly, and ducked down, realizing she probably needed to look lower.

"Jackpot," she whispered, regretting it as soon as she did. "I'm sorry. It's okay."

Fifi bent to her knees and ducked her head to make herself seem smaller and less intimidating.

"You're okay. I won't hurt you." With a soft voice, she moved closer to the baby. She'd found it tucked under the tall brush she'd been eyeing. "Doc's here. He'll help you."

Without hesitation, she scooped the deer up and cradled it in her lap while it shook ferociously.

"Doc?" she said a little louder, trying to call for help. "Doc, I found it."

Her voice raised, and she cradled it harder as tears began to spill. "Doc. Over here. Doc!"

Ellie heard Fifi first and hollered for Doc and Dawson as they all quickly moved in.

"Slow down," Fifi said. "She's scared. And very hurt. Don't frighten her anymore."

Doc reached Fifi and stared at her with amazement. "You picked it up? Why would you pick it up? You don't know if it's sick, hurt, covered in ticks…"

"I don't know. She's so tiny," Fifi chided. "I just…did it. I felt like she needed a hug…or something. She's so scared, and her poor little face is bleeding. Her leg looks…wrong too."

"She?" Dawson questioned with a smirk.

"Yes, I guess. She seems like a…*she*. I don't know!" Fifi cried, raising her gaze to Doc. "Can you help her? Please tell me you can help her."

Doc extended a hand to inspect the baby deer, but it began to squirm. "Whoa. You're all right."

"Shhh, you're okay," Fifi said as she began to rock the deer still sitting under the brush. The deer calmed.

Doc raised his brow and turned to Dawson, offering a shrug.

"I think she likes you, Miss Fifi," Ellie said. "I think you get to keep her now."

"Let's not get ahead of ourselves," Doc said, afraid the deer was too badly injured. "But I do think it's taken to you for some reason. Let's get it back to the barn and check it over. See if there's anything we can do."

When he reached for the animal, it began to squirm again. "All right, looks like you're carrying it."

"I can do that," Fifi said with a sniffle. "But maybe help me up? My arms are sort of…full."

Dawson and Doc each hooked an arm under Fifi from behind where the deer couldn't see them and lifted her to her feet. They flanked either side, helping her back through the woods to Doc's truck.

"Do you think it's one of Santa's reindeer?" Ellie asked. "Maybe it's here for the festival and just got lost?"

Fifi smiled. "You know what? I bet you're right. We better hurry and get her back to the barn and fixed up so she's ready for next week."

"Fiona," Doc warned, worried Fifi was getting the little girl's hopes up.

"You'll fix her, Doc. She'll be fine." Fifi smiled through the tears. "You can do it."

Doc ran his hand through his hair, feeling the weight of the situation. Not only had Fifi fallen for a baby deer she'd just met, but the kid wrapped it up into the whole Christmas and Santa Claus thing. If he *couldn't* help it, he would certainly break Fifi's heart and ruin Christmas forever for the little girl. No pressure.

"Let's get going and see what we're dealing with and what we can do about it." Doc said, "I'll shoot you a text later, Dawson, and let you know how it goes."

"I'll prepare my *story* now, just in case," Dawson whispered to Doc, realizing how severe the animal's injuries could be.

"That's probably a good idea," Doc replied before hopping in his truck and driving off.

* * *

"Well, now we just wait," Doc said, drying off his hands. "I can't believe you sat out here this long."

Fifi smiled. "I wanted to make sure she was okay. Besides, Dallas is still out here. He kept me company."

"The sloth kept you company?"

"You'd be surprised. He's a good listener." Fifi grinned.

"That I don't doubt. Well, you were right. It's a female. She's a little small, so I'm guessing she's either a late spring birth or a runt."

"And her mom?" Fifi asked.

"There's no telling. She could have been hit; poachers could have nailed her. In fact, running out of the woods like this little one did and right into a rig, she was scared."

"Running from something?"

"Maybe? Deer do weird crap all the time. That's why they get hit. But babies tend to be more timid and stay back, hide."

"Poor Jane," Fifi said, looking in the stall.

"Jane? Who's Jane?" Doc looked around, confused.

"Jane Doe. My baby deer," Fifi said. "While you were working on her, I looked up deer facts on my phone with Dallas. We learned females are does, so it only made sense to name her Jane Doe."

"Yeah, only name that makes sense," Doc said sarcastically with an eye roll. "What did Dallas think of the name?"

Fifi tossed him a cross look. "He's a *sloth*. He doesn't have an opinion. You okay, Bain?"

"Your Hollywood is showing. Fifi," he said. "*Jane* is in shock, underweight, and maybe a little malnourished. She has a broken leg, and her face is the equivalent of a bad bloody nose and a black eye. The injuries aren't critical, but the other stuff could be. She's done with the poking and prodding for the day. So, we'll see how she does through the night. I have her on an IV to take care of the big things, and a little extra something to keep her calm so she can rest."

"She'll be fine. I can stay with her."

Doc raised his brow. "You realize this is just a fancy barn, right? You sure you want to sleep in it?"

"I used to sleep out here when I was a kid, and it was just a beatdown old barn back then," Fifi said. "I'm only half Hollywood, Doc."

"Well, I'm on tonight. My techs are off since they're covering most of next week while we take care of the festival commitments. I'll go grab some food and drinks, and we can do what we veterinarians like to call *an all-nighter*."

"You know that's like a common thing, right? I mean, it isn't exclusive to your kind, Doc," Fifi teased. "And I'm feeling pizza from the Ponderosa."

"One large pizza and plenty of caffeine coming up," he said.

11

MONDAY

THE FOURTH OF JULY CAME AND WENT, BRINGING ONE HOLIDAY festival to an end while the other was just getting started. When Fifi wasn't in town helping the volunteers shift from one holiday to the next, she was at home with Jane Doe in the barn while she continued to work on her passion project, which she'd finished.

Only three days had passed, yet so much had happened in that short time. Life in slow motion was new to Fifi, and she didn't hate it. Spending time in the barn with Jane Doe meant even more time with Doc. She didn't hate that either. They'd stayed up the first night with Jane Doe talking about everything and nothing. It was comfortable — it was pleasant. Surprise...she didn't hate *that* either.

"We got a full mailbag," Doc said as he entered the grange hall. "Those kids didn't waste any time filling the 'letters to Santa' mailbox. It's been out...what, a little over twenty-four hours?"

"Do you guys always get that many?" Fifi asked the others on the letters to Santa committee.

"Oh, we get more letters than we have kids in this town,"

Lou said. "Some of them write handfuls because they remember something they wanted to add or see someone in need and hope Santa can help them out."

"That's so sweet," Fifi said. "And you guys write back to all of them?"

"Sure do," Lou said. "That's why we have such a big committee. We keep the letters short, sweet, and always sign off with your elf name."

"Elf name?" Fifi questioned.

"Well, you already have yourself an elf name with Fifi, but it's also a bit of a giveaway." Lou laughed. "Better pick something else, and *Glitter Tits* isn't family-friendly…or so I'm told."

Fifi smiled. "Twinkle McJingle."

"That was fast." Doc chuckled.

"I did the set for a Christmas movie. Well, it was a whole franchise. Like three movies." Fifi shrugged.

"Yeah, we heard about it. Dee credited you for the entire multimillion-dollar box office hit thing," Lou said. "She said *if it wasn't so beautiful to look at, it wouldn't have been worth a dime*."

Fifi laughed at Lou's impression, which was oddly close to her grandmother's voice. "She was pretty proud of that one. I actually won multiple awards for it. Gram was the first person I called."

"From the awards show, if I recall correctly," Lou said. "We were all sittin' around her livin' room watchin' it live. Dee had us all dress up and called it a viewin' party."

"Really? I had no idea you were all there, and she went to all that trouble," Fifi replied.

"Said you were the best, and one day, if you ever found your way back home to McKenzie, we'd have the best festivals and parades with you at the helm." Lou shared. "Said Arrow Springs never stood a chance against you."

Fifi thought about what a life in McKenzie might look like. She'd spoken about it every summer with her grandmother as a girl, but as an adult, the appeal was different. Or was it? She was used to a fast pace and liked to stay busy, and though McKenzie kept things interesting at the moment, what would happen when there wasn't a festival to curate or a deer to rescue?

Fifi's novel was complete, and if it proceeded as she planned, completing the series could keep her busy, but that was her passion project. There was no way to know if it would be enough. If it wasn't, going back to LA wasn't necessarily an option. It had taken her years to get where she was, and it wasn't necessarily something she could simply walk back into down the road — she'd have to start over. Showbiz was a crapshoot at best.

The risk was too great, and fun in the moment didn't translate to a lifetime in Mayberry. Small-town living would get old, the silly committees for everything would become ridiculous, and all the meddling annoying. Just wait until winter hit with days of snow on end. Life had to become monotonous at that point. And all the animals, though they were wearing on her, surely would become overwhelming. There was definitely a difference between visiting and residing in a place. Temporary was fun, permanent was... well, *permanent*.

"Hey, McJingle," Doc said, handing Fifi an envelope from the mailbag. "This letter has your name on it."

"How can that be? I literally just created Twinkle McJingle," Fifi questioned. "Don't tell me it's a magic mailbag."

"No. It says *Fifi* on it." He shrugged. "You know this is

all made up, right? No magic bag? Have you been sippin' on Lou's flask over there?"

"It's medicinal," Lou chided.

Fifi tossed Doc a dirty look and opened the letter.

DEAR FIFI,
I've liked you since I met you…
Maybe before…
-Santa

"WELL, WHAT'S IT SAY?" LOU ASKED.

Fifi read it aloud, smiling through every word. "Isn't that sweet? I wonder who would write something like that. It wasn't you, was it, Lou?"

"Honey, that sounds more like a love note, and I already have a sweetheart of my own," Lou said. "And you're too young and not my type."

"A love note? You think?" Fifi looked around the room, searching for answers. "But who? I haven't really been here long enough for an admirer."

"The answer is in the note, dear. It says *maybe before*. Who's known ya since before you were here?" Lou asked.

"Honestly, half the town knew me as a kid, and the rest have said they feel like they know me because my gram talked everyone's ear off about me, come to find out."

"She really did talk about you a lot," Doc interrupted. "You've always been the elusive celebrity around these parts."

"Huh. The mailbox has been out for more than a day, so it really could have been anyone." Fifi held the letter to her chest. "No matter who it is, it's very sweet. Even if it isn't a *love note*."

"Sounds like you have a bit of a fan club here," Doc said.

"Yeah. Maybe. Too bad I'm not staying," Fifi said, her smile suddenly dim.

"No one's kickin' ya out, kid. Maybe you should rethink the leavin' thing," Lou added. "Maybe this here's a sign. What's really waitin' for ya back in Holly-weird?"

"Only my whole life." Fifi snorted. "Nah. I do love it here, and I'm going to miss it. But it's not where I belong."

"Then that's that," Bain said. "These letters aren't going to write themselves, and tonight is the first night of the festival. We need to get these over to the ladies running Santa's post office station to sort."

Fifi smiled and put her pen to paper, but her mind was somewhere else entirely. What if Lou had been right and someone really did have feelings for her? Even if it wasn't a love note, and just a friendly one, it spoke volumes about what she was willing to leave behind. The only anonymous note she'd received in Los Angeles was one apologizing for sideswiping her car and one telling her she parked like an asshole. That would never happen here.

12

TUESDAY

"It's been bugging me ever since I read it," Fifi said. "What if Lou was right? What if it wasn't just a friendly note, but a *love note*, as she called it?"

Doc shrugged his shoulders, listening while he helped sort the finished letters to the kids, alphabetically, into the makeshift *Santa's Post Office*. "Would it make a difference if it was one or the other? I mean seriously, would you stay if you knew it was someone with *feelings* for you?"

"I mean…maybe?" Fifi said.

Doc gave her a hard-knowing stare. "You've been counting down the days until you can leave. Your life is back in LA, remember?"

"Yeah. It really is. I'm just really stumped. I wish—" Fifi stopped. "I wish I *knew*. I really do love it here, but I just can't justify giving up everything I've worked so hard for… for…for…who knows what this is?"

"Work. Your work is there. What if your passion project turns into more than that?" Bain asked. "Would that change anything? I guess what I'm saying is you need to decide what you're working for and what you're working toward. If the movie thing is what you want, then there's your answer. If writing is what you want...well, you can do that anywhere. Right?"

"Writing really is my passion and why I got into the industry like I did — to open doors," Fifi reasoned.

"And how is that going for you — any doors open?" Bain questioned.

"No, not yet. But in all fairness, I haven't tried any," Fifi admitted.

"Why?"

"Fear, I guess? Fear of rejection? I know I'm good at my job, hands down. I have the awards and income to prove it. But writing? It's exposing myself in a different way and leaves me vulnerable. It's personal."

"But what if it's great? You can't always play it safe," Bain replied. "You sent it off to your friend, or whatever, right?"

"I did. It'll be a while before I hear back. She has to read it, and she's busy...I'm not holding my breath."

"Hey, Fifi?" a woman interrupted. "I came across a letter with your name on it while sorting them out."

"You did?" Fifi's mood suddenly improved. "It was in your stack?"

"Yep. With all the letters to the kids." The woman handed it over.

Fifi set her stack of envelopes down and inspected the outside of the letter. It looked just like all the others — and just like the one from yesterday. She smacked it against her hand, contemplating whether to open it right then and there while she looked at Doc, who shrugged, as if he knew what she was quietly asking.

"Open it," he said. "Maybe you'll have your answer. Friend or admirer."

Before he finished his sentence, she was ripping into the red envelope, tossing it aside while she unfolded the Christmas stationery inside.

DEAR FIFI,
Your smile can light up a thousand rooms...
-Santa

"HUH," SHE SAID. "NOT SURE WHAT TO MAKE OF THAT."

"Did I hear there was another one of them notes?" Lou came rushing in.

"Wow, small-town gossip spreads quickly around here." Fifi laughed. "Yeah. Another one. Here, read it." Fifi handed the letter to Lou.

"It's a man, honey. You have yourself a man."

"Whoa. I don't have anything. Even if it is a man, he isn't mine. And what if it's just a friendly statement? Nothing more, nothing less. Kind words only," Fifi rebutted. "What's your take, Doc?"

"Don't drag me into this. I have no clue." Doc put his hands up in surrender. "I think it could go either way."

"Yeah." Fifi took the letter back from Lou and stared at it for a moment. "It's definitely a man's handwriting. Too sloppy to be a woman's."

"On behalf of all men, I'm offended," Doc joked.

Fifi elbowed him. "Oh please. It's a fact. Get over it. There has to be a way to figure this out."

"How do I look?" Fifi heard a deep voice in the distance that had her attention.

"That's it." Fifi jumped off the table she'd been sitting on. "There's the clue. Santa!"

When the man in the Santa suit pulled down his beard and yanked off the hat, she saw who was hiding behind the jolly laugh.

"It's literally Santa. Well, Dawson. I'll just ask," Fifi said, heading toward the man in the suit.

"Whoa," Doc said. "I don't think it's—"

"Oh, come on," Fifi interrupted. "I'm a modern woman. Why not cut to the chase?"

Lou cleared her throat. "No, I think what Doc's tryin' to say is—"

With a dramatic eye roll, Fifi stepped away from her friends. "Seriously, you two… I got this."

Fifi made her way across the room despite Lou and Doc right behind her trying to regain her attention.

"Dawson, hi," she said, pulling his attention from the woman he was talking to.

"Fifi," Dawson replied. "Good to see you. I heard the deer…er, Jane Doe is doing good. That's great."

"Yeah. She's amazing. Getting better each day," Fifi agreed. "Anyway, I had a question for you."

Fifi held up the letter, but before she could say a word, Doc interrupted.

"Hey, Sam." Doc turned to Fifi with a wide-eyed stare. "Fifi, have you met Dawson's *wife*, Sam, yet?"

Sam extended her hand and offered a friendly smile. "Fifi. I've heard so much about you. Our daughter, Ellie, has been talking about the lady who saved Santa's reindeer for days now. You're basically a hero to our kids."

"*Kids*? Like more than one? Wow." Fifi wasn't sure what to say to talk her way out of the humiliation brewing. "You guys must be busy. That's great. Yeah. Great to meet you too. Wow, Ellie. What a sweet girl. So, married? That's amazing."

She was on an endless loop of pure ramble, trying to pull

her foot out of her mouth and climb her way out of the hole she'd been digging.

"Thanks." Dawson nodded. "Never a dull moment at our house. I'm needed at the town center in a minute. What was your question?"

"Question?" Fifi was starting to sweat. She could only imagine the shade of crimson gracing her cheeks. "Oh, um. How's your...truck? I mean, the dent. From the deer. Oh, and your daughter. I was, you know, curious. But it sounds like she's just fine. Cute kid. But yeah...you might want to get out there. I hear there's a good line today. Here's to no one peeing on...your...lap."

Sam and Dawson laughed, though it was more of a courtesy laugh. If this conversation was anything, it was awkward.

Doc put his hand on the small of Fifi's back and began to guide her back to their sorting station. "You weren't kidding when you said six shots of espresso makes you chatty."

"Oh, yep. Whew," Fifi said, wiping the sweat from her brow. "I won't be doing *that* again."

Lou laughed out loud. "Makin' a darn fool of yourself, girl. But it's mighty entertaining."

"Thanks...Lou." Fifi nodded, then disappeared to her station and began to sort.

Lou came up behind her. "We tried to warn ya."

"Well, a little faster next time. And six shots of espresso? I'd never—"

"They don't know that," Doc argued. "You were sounding more like six shots of whiskey. You're welcome."

"That was probably the most embarrassing thing I've ever done. I mean...he's literally in a Santa suit. It made sense."

"Oh, honey. The Santa changes every night." Lou chuckled. "If it was one of the Santas...well, it could be any number of 'em."

"That's it. Who has the Santa sign-up?" Fifi asked.

"Nobody knows. It was always kept a secret. Dee had it," Doc said.

"Hmm...it's probably with that notebook I never found, and the orders for the festival I never found," Fifi reasoned. "This could drag out all week."

"Well, not necessarily. We can mark the Christmas Eve Santa off your list. It's the same guy every year," Doc added. "Old man Tilly."

"Is he that old he wouldn't be sending love-slash-friendship notes to the new girl in town?"

"Yeah, and because he's afraid of Mrs. Tilly." Doc laughed.

"Okay. So, it isn't the first or the last Santa," Fifi said. "That leaves like five other Santas. We just need to wait it out...or wait for a better clue...or sign."

13

WEDNESDAY

"Doc, come quick," a man said. "It's Lucy…she's at it again."

"Ah, crap. Poor thing," Doc said, tossing his stack of letters from the elves on a nearby table.

Fifi looked around, watching a crowd follow out of the grange hall, and decided to see what the fuss was about.

"Who's Lucy?" she asked Lou.

"Oh, that poor thing. Her baby was taken from her. She's not been right since."

"Her baby? That's awful," Fifi said.

"Yeah, she starts spitting on everyone, hollering around town, chasing people. It's hard to watch," Lou said.

"Yet everyone is running to the scene…to watch. You'd think she'd get a little grace, and people would let her have her dignity, not eat popcorn while they watch her world fall apart," Fifi defended.

"Oh, honey, it ain't that dramatic." Lou laughed as they reached the town center. "Sometimes, it's a hoot to watch. She's all spit and vinegar. Sweet as can be one minute, then sour as can be the next."

"I would think having your child taken from you would…" Fifi stopped midsentence when the commotion unfolding in front of her had her eating her own words.

"Lou? Is Lucy…?"

Lou cackled and slapped her leg. "A llama? Yes, dear. She is. Look at her go."

"What is a llama doing in the town center? Did she escape or something?"

"Well, I'd imagine she escaped the live nativity scene."

"I don't recall a llama in the live nativity. I thought the animals were just props. And isn't it a camel…with the wise men? I've never read about the baby Jesus and his…llama."

"Oh, honey. Where we gonna get a camel around here? Use your imagination. Ole Tommy brings Lucy to town every year to stand in and play the role of the camel, but ever since he and Jenny split, it's been nothin' but llama drama."

"I thought it was because her baby was taken away."

"Well, it was. When Jenny left, she got the baby. Tommy got to keep Lucy. That animal went stark raving mad. Tommy tried to win custody in court but lost. Then he tried to buy Vince—"

"Vince?" Fifi questioned.

"Vince…Lucy's baby. Keep up, honey. Anywho, Jenny wouldn't take his money. The city council got involved due to all the complaints, but there was nothin' they could do. So, the town came together and pooled all their money, even used the city's rainy-day fund to try to get that baby back for Lucy. Jenny said she'd rather watch Tommy suffer than take the money…She's as crazy as the damn llama. Do you know how much money this town raised? We've got ourselves a billionaire livin' one property over from Tommy and gets the brunt of Lucy's tantrums."

"Wow. That's awful."

"Yep. Llama drama. I mean, look at her go. Ever been spit on by one of them things? It's nastier than a cow pie in the summer. Whew." Lou clutched her chest, a disgusted look on her face. "You won't be able to eat for a day or two after Lucy gets ya."

"Why'd they come get Doc?" Fifi asked. "How does he help?"

"He talks her down."

"Talks…to the llama. Like reasons with her, or…what?"

Lou gave Fifi an odd look. "You feelin' okay? It's a llama. She doesn't speak English. He just gets her to calm down with one of them pills or sometimes a shot in the rear when she ain't lookin'. Boy, that gets her goin' for a minute."

Fifi pushed her way through the crowd and stood next to Doc while he opened a black canvas bag and prepared a syringe.

"You might want to stay back. This is one of her bad fits. I'll have to inject her, then take her back to the barn for observation until the tranquilizer wears off to see how her mood is."

"Doc, I think this is it. I think it's time to find her a sanctuary or maybe put her down," a man said.

"You must be Tommy?" Fifi asked.

"That's me," he said.

"She just wants to be a mama," Fifi said.

"Lucy has gone too far this time. I mean, look at her! She has hostages!" Tommy said.

"It's just so sad." Her eyes filled with tears as she watched the raging llama spit on everyone she had trapped in the live nativity, even the baby Jesus.

"It is. I haven't a clue what to do for her," Doc Bain said, ignoring Tommy. "Animals from that species don't emotionally bond like that. They have herd mentality, but they don't have an emotional crisis when a family member moves on. I've reached out to experts, but there's not a single case of a llama having an emotional breakdown or suffering from severe depression over the loss of a baby."

Fifi's eyes lit up. "You're brilliant, Doc."

"Thanks? I think?"

"You still have the horse trailer hooked up to the truck. Go back it up to the nativity."

"And?" Doc Bain wasn't sure how this was going to help.

"Instead of drugging her and dragging her in, let her choose. She hasn't had a say in any of this. Tommy and Jenny have had all the say."

Doc looked around, unsure where she was coming from and where all this was going. "That's because she's a llama. They don't care what we say or do."

"Exactly. She doesn't care that Tommy and Jenny are too selfish to see what's best for her or…Victor."

"Hey, who you calling selfish?" Tommy chided. "If anyone's selfish, it's Jenny, takin' that baby and putting my misery above money."

"Well, it's not like you offered Lucy to Jenny so she could be with Victor again." Fifi shrugged. "Two-way street, Tommy."

"Whatever. She doesn't want her. Doesn't even want the baby. She's sellin' it to some breeder in Portland." Tommy stormed off.

"Who is Victor?" Bain asked.

"Her baby!"

"Oh, *Vince*," he corrected.

Fifi shook her head. "Whatever. Victor? Vince? The point is, she isn't acting like a typical animal, so don't treat her like one. She just wants someone to listen to her. I've been to enough therapy in my life to know that as fact. So, let's listen."

"Truck's right over there. I'll just back it up to the nativity," Bain said. "What've we got to lose at this point?"

"Hey, Fifi? Fifi…" Jed Baker hollered. "This was with the letters. It has your name on it."

"Another letter…" Fifi whispered, staring at the red envelope before slipping it into her back pocket. "Thanks, Jed."

"Of course. Word's gettin' out. Rumor has it, you're dating Santa." Jed giggled.

"Your guess is as good as mine. I wish I knew what these were about," she admitted before turning her attention back to the horse trailer backing its way in her direction.

A little coaxing with hay and clapping to stir in her another direction, and the duo was able to get Lucy the llama into the horse trailer voluntarily…sans any sedatives. The crowd cheered when they pulled away, and the three wise men went home to shower while Mary and Joseph found a clean Jesus. There was plenty to do for the festival, but Fifi left Lou in charge, certain she and the volunteers could handle it all without her as they had every year.

When Doc backed the trailer up to the barn, he finally asked, "What now, Dr. Gallagher?"

"Doctor?" Fifi laughed.

"Doctor of psychology," Bain teased. "Looney bin for the girl in the back or what?"

"I was actually thinking we'd give her a baby."

"Except one of the only animals I *don't* have here is a baby llama. Next idea?"

"I was thinking maybe any baby would do?" Fifi was hesitant to offer her idea. Now that they were actually there, she wasn't sure it was a good one. "Jane Doe could use a mom, so I thought maybe…they'd help each other?"

Doc sat back, resting his chin on his propped fist, and stared at Fifi while he thought it out. "Worst case, it doesn't work. Either way, they need to get acclimated to one another because if I heard him right, Tommy just surrendered his animal to us."

"I heard it too." Fifi snickered. "You're the proud new owner of the llama drama. You're welcome."

"Let's move Jane Doe to a companion stall, then unload Lucy in the one next door. They'll be nice and close, able to interact, but the gate between them will keep Jane Doe protected if Lucy loses her shit again. You're cleaning her if Lucy spits on her, though."

"Deal." Fifi laughed.

They opted to stay in the barn and observe the two for the night — something they seemed to be making a habit of. Dinner was covered when various townspeople dropped by with everything from homemade casseroles to food from town. Everyone was curious to see what the latest news was on the llama drama.

"I almost forgot." Fifi reached into her back pocket and pulled out the red envelope. "Santa drama."

DEAR FIFI,
You deserve the world…
-Santa

"SOUNDS SERIOUS," DOC SAID.

"Right? I just don't understand."

"What's not to understand?"

Fifi paused. "I don't understand what they mean? So, say it's an admirer…what's the point here? What's the message?

Everyone knows I'm leaving, so what's the point of these? Maybe they're just kind gestures, like affirmations to make me feel good or something?"

"Could be." Doc shrugged. "Maybe you're just overthinking things."

"Or maybe I'm underthinking them. There's a message here, right?"

"Clearly." Doc snorted.

"No. I mean a message for me. I'm supposed to do something with this, but…what? Go home happy? Why would someone waste their time on that…on a stranger, really?"

"Something tells me that's part of the message for you to…figure it all out."

"Maybe… I just wish there was something more here, something to go off of."

"You mean like a sign?" Doc teased.

"Yes, actually. A sign. For what, I don't know."

14

THURSDAY

"Good morning," Doc said as Fifi finally raised her head.

"Is it morning already?"

"You fell asleep around midnight. Snored all night long."

Fifi tossed her makeshift pillow at Doc. "I don't snore."

"How would you know? You're sleeping."

"Because I know." She laughed. "Have you been up all night?"

"Most of it. I took a couple of power naps in there, though."

"You must be exhausted," Fifi said, stretching her legs as she stood.

"I'm used to it."

"I was going to offer to make the coffee, but it smells like you already did." Fifi moved to the kitchenette and raised a mug as her way of asking if he'd like a cup.

"Jed's already been here with fresh pastries. Said they're all your favorites, compliments of the town for rescuing Lucy's hostages yesterday."

"That's really sweet and thoughtful. The sad thing is, all I

Christmas in July

can think about right now is he saw me sleeping in here with you, and the whole town is likely buzzing about it right now." Fifi shook her head.

"Jed's not really part of that scene. Besides, if he's spreading anything, it's new drama llama."

"Oh, no." Fifi's heart sank. "What happened? It didn't work, did it? I should have known better. It was a bad idea."

"Hey, don't sell yourself short. Come take a look."

Fifi approached the stall door and couldn't believe what she saw.

"After three hours straight of those two leaning against each other through the gate, I thought it was safe to take down the barrier. They've been curled up together like that ever since."

"I can't believe it worked! Look at them, Doc!" Fifi threw her arms around Doc in excitement.

His arms wrapped around her waist, sharing the excitement, and he lifted her from the ground. When he put her back down, she dropped her arms and bit her bottom lip, realizing how carried way she'd just gotten.

"I guess they just needed each other," she said softly.

"Yeah. It appears so. Good call," he said. "We'll have to label you our new town animal whisperer. The gray squirrels have been playing chicken a lot lately…see what you can find out there. Deep abandonment issues leading them to risky behavior that gives them a satisfying thrill, albeit a short one?"

Fifi smacked his arm. "Ha. Funny."

She opened the pastry box and let out a gasp. "Doc, it's a letter…in the donuts."

"What?"

"There's a letter…in the pastry box. Jed brought the pastry box, right?"

Doc shook his head. "Yeah, but he's married...happily, I might add."

"I know," she said with an ounce of sadness. "Then maybe they aren't *love notes* and just kind words from Jed. I mean, he has known me since I was little, always been kind to me, and felt terrible they had to miss my gram's memorial."

"Could be. He *is* a really nice guy. Read it. See what it says."

Dear Fifi,

I'm already afraid to lose you, and you're not even mine...stay?

-Santa

"That's not from Jed." Doc laughed.

Fifi's eyes were wide. Her jaw dropped. "I don't know what to say. This is...It's..."

"Serious?" Doc finished her thought for her.

"Very serious. Someone wants me to stay...here...in McKenzie."

"I kind of gathered that from the note." Doc chuckled.

"But who? This is the part that always stumps me. Who knows me well enough to want me to stay? It has to be someone who's known me longer than this trip. Someone from when I was a kid, right?"

Doc put his hands up. "Beats me. You're the one with all the therapy experience."

"This changes everything."

"Meaning you're going to stay?" Doc asked.

"No. I mean, how could I? This is sweet, but I don't know

who this is from. It could be someone, you know…a little sketchy."

"Good point. Got a list of potential admirers? I know how your mind works, so there's got to be at least a few candidates?"

"Actually, no," Fifi said as her mind began to wander.

15

FRIDAY

"So beautiful," Doc whispered, looking Fifi's way.

With her back against the stall holding Lucy and Jane Doe, she stiffened at Doc's words and burning gaze. "Um, excuse me?"

"Lucy and Jane Doe. Nature. It's just…beautiful. Right?" Bain said, seeming to look past Fifi.

Fifi's cheeks began to blush. "Oh. Them. Yeah. It really is. I thought you were…I mean, I thought you meant…never mind."

She closed her eyes and walked off in embarrassment, tripping over the blanket she'd slept on while camping out with her two newly found furry friends. Fifi fell forward, knocking her head on an open stall door.

"Jesus, Fifi. Are you all right?" Doc asked, rushing to her side.

She pushed herself up to her knees and sat there, cradling her head.

"Let me see it, darlin'. That was a pretty good hit."

Doc examined her head, then rushed into the exam room and returned with supplies. "Pressure to stop the bleeding and ice for the swelling."

"Bleeding?"

"Shhh. You're okay. It's a superficial wound...that means surface. But there's already a bump forming, so the ice will help manage that. I'm worried about a concussion, though."

"Concussion? But I have to get to town soon. There are the letters to the kids and—"

Doc placed his hands on her shoulders, commanding her attention. "It will all get done. Those guys have been doing it for years, so they know what to do. I'll make a couple of quick calls, and it'll be handled. Meanwhile, you hang out here with me where I can keep an eye on that bump and make sure you don't start acting weird."

"So, am I officially part of your stray rescue now?" she teased.

"Yep. And since *your* new residents need supervision too, I think I'll keep you out here with them."

"In the barn. With the animals. You're really taking this Hollywood stray thing to the extreme."

He laughed. "Don't worry. I have this place set up for long-term stays. A person could actually live out here."

"This ought to be good," Fifi said, crossing her arms, waiting to be impressed.

"Take a seat on that big pillow chair thing. I'll be back," Doc said, disappearing to his office.

Fifi plopped back down on the oversized beanbag she'd now used a couple of times for overnight stays in the barn. It was big enough for two to three people, which was great, but the name was a little cringy — it was called a *Lovesac*. It was such a *guy thing* to have, but it made sense in the barn because, despite its size, it was still portable and could be moved to wherever Doc, or one of his techs, needed it for those cases that required round-the-clock care. A folding chair just wouldn't be the same.

"You ready for this?" Doc hollered from around the corner.

"Depends. If it's a saddle, harness, or anything else that's *weird*...I'm out of here."

"I have something better than that," he said, his backside coming into view.

"That doesn't make me feel any better."

Doc pulled a large flat-screen TV on a stand with wheels around the corner and parked it right in front of the *Lovesac*. "Movie day."

"M'kay? I like where this is going."

He held up the remote and hit a few buttons. "Since it's Christmas in *July,* I thought we could do a Christmas movie marathon. It's all on demand."

Fifi couldn't help but chuckle. It was a little ridiculous but still sweet and completely thoughtful.

"Maybe one of your movies will be on this thing," he said, clicking through the selection.

"Oh, I hope not. When I'm done with a project...I'm *done.*"

Though her words weren't referring to anything specifically, they both felt a sharp pang from them. After all, the Christmas festival, cleaning out Dee's house, and McKenzie Ridge were all just projects. For Fifi, the words stung. For Doc Bain, they were just a reminder.

"Yeah. Well, we can watch whatever you want. It doesn't even have to be Christmas," Doc said, his enthusiasm a little less prominent.

"I love the idea of Christmas movies all day in a barn while it's ninety-plus degrees outside in the middle of summer. It's perfect. The only thing missing is cocoa with marshmallows, but…it's *ninety degrees outside*."

Doc paused for a moment, then said, "I'll be back. Don't go anywhere."

Fifi heard the truck start up and chuckled. Who knew what this man was up to, but she couldn't wait to find out. He was full of surprises today. Taking his instructions seriously, she didn't go anywhere. She snuggled into the *Lovesac* and watched Lucy and Jane Doe wander their joint stall while snacking on hay.

She pulled the red envelope from her back pocket and re-read the last Santa letter she'd received. Hanging on the word *stay*, she thought about the possibility. Only a few short weeks ago, she couldn't wait to get back to LA and start on her next movie set, but now, it just felt like work, an obligation, and less like *home*. Unfortunately, it *was* home, and she *was* obligated to go back because it *was* work, which translated to income, which meant her bills would be paid.

There were too many uncertainties in McKenzie. Her skills weren't exactly marketable in a tourist town, and working for the local Stop and Shop wouldn't provide the means she needed to maintain half the lifestyle she was accustomed to. Dee had left her a modest financial inheritance that would help in the immediate future, but it wouldn't sustain her or the property long-term. It was all too risky.

Besides, she couldn't hang her entire future on the request of a stranger, even if it was Santa. She laughed at the idea. As romantic as it was, who made such dramatic life decisions on letters from Santa? A Santa she didn't know, and who couldn't have known her — or known her well anyway.

Fifi looked at her watch when the rumbling of tires on the gravel road caught her attention.

"Wow, that was fast," she said to herself. "Doc must not have gone far."

When an unfamiliar face walked in, holding a cat, she took to her feet. "Hey."

The seemingly kind man with smoldering eyes, chiseled features, and a beautiful olive complexion gave Fifi a blinding mega-watt smile. He...was...*handsome*.

"Hey. Aren't you Fiona Gallagher?" he said.

"Yeah...well, Fifi. Have we...*met*?"

"Yes and no. Gabe Hernandez. I work over at the fire station."

"You're a firefighter. How noble." She cringed, unsure where that came from or why she'd said it.

"Uh...something like that." Gabe chuckled. "Is Doc around?"

"Actually, you just missed him, but I think he'll be back shortly. He doesn't have anyone else here, so I can't imagine him leaving more than a few minutes. He ran to town I think?"

"Well, maybe you can help me then. I'm in a bit of a rush, but promised to drop this guy...or gal...off. I just pulled her out of a burning building. It was one of those life or death things — and I risked it all for the cat. Got her out just before the whole thing collapsed. It was tense, but we made it out."

"Oh my gosh, are you serious? That's incredible."

"Nah, I was just trying to impress you. Did it work?"

"For a minute, yes."

"Good. It's actually been roaming around the station, howling and moaning. The guys said it's in heat and since I'm the only single one in the bunch, they thought it'd be funny to make her my *problem*."

"Wow, that's...*weird*." Fifi laughed.

"Right? That's what I deal with over there. Anyway, I

don't know how to tell if a cat's in heat or if it's hurt…or just pissed off or something, but I figured Doc would know what to do," Gabe said.

"I'm sure he would. Um, I'm not sure where to put her, though, and I'd hate for her to run off. I'll just hold her. She seems sweet enough, and if she isn't, I happen to know where Doc stashes the food, so…"

"You wouldn't mind?" Gabe's eyes lit up. "You'd be a lifesaver. I need to get to the town center and get the costume on. It's going to be murder wearing that suit in this heat with kids climbing all over me."

"You're…Santa?" Fifi said in a near whisper.

"I mean, not the real Santa." Gabe laughed. "But I guess you can call me one of his helpers."

"So, you're tonight's Santa? That's…*great*!"

"Thank you? I'm actually tomorrow night's Santa, but we just took a call at pavilion park. It turns out, tonight's Santa went a little heavy on the lemonade. The vodka he was doctoring it up with didn't mesh well with the heat. So, he's sleeping it off, and I'm filling in."

"That's really sweet of you." Fifi admired. "And you're single…too? I mean, not that it makes a difference or anything, just saying that…well… So, let me take that cat for you."

Gabe grinned and handed her the cat.

"Whoa. You sure she doesn't belong to anyone? She doesn't seem to be skipping any meals." Fifi cringed at how awkward that must have come across.

"Pretty sure. She's been roaming the station a good week. Nobody seems to be missing her."

"Doc will figure it out and probably put her on a diet. He's really big on animal health and wellness…and you really don't care about all that." Fifi shook her head in embarrassment.

"Nah, it's all right. Doc's a good guy. I trust him with her. But I do need to get going so I'm not late for the kids. We good here?"

"Yep. Good. Here. We gooood." She was doing it again. It was like she couldn't control herself, and the odd tone she was using was even more embarrassing than her inability to carry a normal conversation with a handsome man — a handsome man who also may be her Santa.

Gabe turned to leave, but not before he said, "I remember you, growing up. You'd spend the summers here with Dee, right?"

Her eyes lit up. He *did* know her. "Yeah. That was me."

"I remember. Always the prettiest girl on the playground."

Fifi's mouth began to move, but nothing came out. It was all starting to fall into place. Handsome firefighter Gabe Hernandez knew her, remembered her, and thought she was pretty…well, when she was twelve anyway, which kind of sounded weird now that he was grown. She was sure he meant pretty then in an age-appropriate way.

"Still are," he said with a wink.

Nope. He's not creepy. He meant it in an age-appropriate way and still thought she was pretty. Score.

"Thanks…"

"You going to the Christmas Eve dance tomorrow night? I mean, I know you are kind of running the whole thing, but do you get to, you know, have fun too?" he asked.

"I am. I mean…" She closed her eyes for a second and got herself together. "I will be there — to have fun."

"Save me a dance?" he asked. "I'll only be there a short time because I have to do the whole Santa thing, but—"

"I'd love to," she said, a little too eager.

"Great. I'll see you then."

And he was gone.

Fifi stood there, rocking the cat she was cradling, trying to wrap her mind around what had just happened. Sexy firefighter was so cliché, but who was she to judge? He'd known her since she was a little kid, knew her gram…what was she supposed to do with this information?

"You okay in here?" Doc said, startling her.

"Oh. Yes. I didn't hear you pull in. You just missed—"

"Gabe, yeah, I passed him on the way in. He said he left me something," Doc said, eyeing the cat she was holding. "It's the cat, isn't it?"

"Yeah, she might be hurt or in heat he said. She's sort of swollen. Maybe she's just overweight?"

Doc laughed. "Or pregnant. That sneaky bastard didn't want her to have her litter at the firehouse."

"Oh, I'm sure he didn't know," Fifi defended. "He's a really nice guy."

"He's a nice guy, but he's also a smart guy and didn't want to deal with the cat…Oh well, she just would have ended up out here anyway since we don't have an official animal shelter."

"He's Santa," Fifi deadpanned.

"Yeah, he volunteers every year. His grandmother makes him."

"No…I mean. He's *the* Santa."

Doc gave her a cross look. "Your head okay? Maybe you hit it a little harder than I thought."

Fifi smacked Doc's arm, then handed him the cat. "I mean the Santa in the letters. It all makes sense. He remembers me from when we were kids, said I was pretty—"

"He said you were pretty? That's a little forward, don't you think?" Doc interrupted.

"No. It wasn't like that. It wasn't weird or anything. He was actually sweet and asked me to save him a dance tomorrow night."

"Wow. Sounds like you have it all figured out," Doc said, looking over the cat.

"Maybe. I guess time will tell." Fifi walked over to the counter where Doc had set down a grocery bag. "So, where did you go?"

"Look in the bag. I got us a few things to hold us over during our Christmas movie marathon. They didn't have hot cocoa at the little market or marshmallows, but I got rocky road ice cream. Thought that was close enough. Call it a frozen hot chocolate if you want."

"I love frozen hot chocolate. This is perfect, Bain," she said, unpacking the bag. "You grabbed sandwiches too. Excellent."

"Yeah, best grinders in town. I got both of your favorites. Figured we could swap halves or something."

"Good idea." Fifi folded the empty bag and set it aside when something caught her eye. Something red. "Doc?"

"Hang on. I'm putting this girl in the nursery. She isn't in heat. She's bitching because she's uncomfortable. She's been in early labor and probably looking for a place to bed down. We're about to have kittens around here, so we'll want to keep an eye on her."

"Are you serious? More babies?"

"Tis the season. She went right to the pile of blankets and started nesting. It's happening," Doc said, meeting her back at the front counter. "So, did you read it? Is it from *Gabe*?"

. . .

DEAR FIFI,
Take a chance…stay?
Love, Santa

"Whoa," she said. "This is…different than the others. Doc, it says *love…love, Santa*?"

Doc shrugged his shoulders. "Does that change anything?"

Fifi hesitated to answer. "I really don't know."

16

SATURDAY

Fifi couldn't believe what a whirlwind the past few days had been. Llama drama, a baby deer, kittens as of last night…it was crazy, but the good kind of crazy. Something was rewarding about being in the midst of everything happening. Then there was the Santa situation.

More conflicted than ever, Fifi laid it all on the line for herself. Maybe Doc was right. He'd said many times that maybe there was a message in all this. That maybe there was more for her than what Hollywood gave her. That she was being pulled in a different direction, and she was ignoring the signs. He also said dreamy Santa letters and fantasies of happily ever after in the mountains didn't pay the bills.

She'd finally decided to lay it all on the line and see where it went. If Gabe was her Santa, then surely she'd know tonight — tomorrow at the latest since she was leaving next week. Why go to all that trouble and not try to stop her from going? That was the sign she needed — a literal one where the man confessing his feeling in short but sweet messages asked her to stay, face-to-face, and gave her a real reason to do so.

If she heard the right words or an opportunity came through that would allow it...she'd stay. If it was really meant to be, the earth would shake, mountains would move, the seas would part, the planets would align, and the universe would flash a big neon sign.

Doc went to the barn for one last check of the animals and to update the tech coming in for the evening. She'd promised to finish up and meet him out there so they could head over to the final night of the festival together. This was the biggest night — their Christmas Eve dance, or faux Christmas Eve.

When she walked in, she was surprised by the handsome man in the suit staring back at her. "Doc."

"Wow," he said. "You look stunning."

Fifi grabbed at the full skirt of her floor-length dress and twirled. "Isn't this great? Can you believe I found this in the spare bedroom closet? It's vintage. Gram must have had this for decades, and it's still perfect."

"Yes, it sure is. I mean...the dress."

"Oh, yeah. I knew what you meant. You clean up pretty good yourself. I thought all you owned was jeans and white T-shirts and those shorts with all the weird pockets."

"Cargo shorts. Yeah, all the pockets come in handy for the job."

"Right," she said. Making her way toward him, she passed Lucy and Jane Doe along the way. "These two seem to be doing great. How about mama and her new babies?"

When she stopped beside him, Doc was speechless as he took in her scent and admired the vision she was.

"Doc?"

"Oh. They're great. All three babies are eating like champs, and mama is a happy girl. I'd say we have another success on our hands. That makes six for you, ya know?"

"Six?"

"Six rescues. You saved Jane Doe from would-be predators in the woods, Lucy from herself, mama cat from the firehouse, and her three babies from…well, the firehouse. All in only a couple of days' time, I might add. I'd say you have a knack for this. If Hollywood doesn't work out, you probably have a solid career in attracting mentally insane and stray animals."

"Ha-ha."

"Oh. I just checked on Dallas too. He'll be ready to travel. Good as new. You can take him in tonight."

"Really?" She clapped her hands, running over to the sloth's log. "What was wrong? Did you ever figure it out?"

"Well, he did his…*business*. And you were right. Looks like he ate a shiny blue rock. It took me a minute, but I found some in one of Dee's candle decorations on one of the tables."

"That little stink." She shook her head. "Wait…for you to know what he ate means you had to look through his…Now, I feel really bad."

"A part of the job. It's shitty sometimes."

"Ohhh, that's a really, really bad joke. Stick to the day job."

Doc laughed and offered his arm. "Shall we?"

"We shall." She hooked her arm through his, and they made their way outside.

"Doc, are we taking the nice truck for a change? I was sort of used to smelling like manure all the time," she joked.

"What can I say? I really know how to treat a lady."

* * *

THE CHRISTMAS EVE DANCE WAS STUNNING. MEGAN SPARKS was in charge of this event every year. As a former New York socialite and party planner extraordinaire, she didn't leave a single thing untouched. It was the perfect balance of red, white, and blue Christmas in the middle of a July heatwave.

Fifi made good on her promise and saved a dance for Gabe. Two, three, six times now, they'd shared a dance. When they weren't dancing, they were talking, catching up, and reminiscing. Doc sat back and watched the whole thing unfold. Fifi had told him she didn't remember Gabe, which made her feel bad, but she seemed to remember him just fine now. Or maybe, she just liked the guy.

It didn't matter to Doc, as long as she was happy. But he did have a problem with Gabe's hand that seemed to be drifting farther and farther down her back. Fifi wasn't that kind of girl, not that Gabe was that kind of guy, but Doc had to draw the line somewhere and would step in and spare them both from the gossip sure to ensue should Gabe's hand become…more intimately placed.

When Fifi got called away to handle an event issue going on *outside* the dance, Doc breathed a little easier. He was going to meet Gabe at the bar and offer a friendly suggestion to keep his hands in the friend zone, but his phone rang, and it was a call he couldn't miss. When he returned, he'd ask Fifi to dance and break up the potential rumor mill that could be starting already.

Unfortunately, the call took a direction Doc was hoping to avoid. Since Fifi was nowhere in sight, he approached Gabe at the bar.

"I can't find Fifi, but I need to go. Got an emergency call…"

Doc went on to explain the nature of the call and asked if Gabe would be able to drive her home in the event he didn't make it back before the night was over. Gabe was happy to oblige.

* * *

When Fifi returned to the party, she scanned the room, locating Gabe rather quickly, but didn't see Doc.

"Hey." She said. "I can't find Doc and need to talk to him."

"He had an emergency. Looks like I get to escort you home tonight. I have to dress up in the suit for the kids, but once that's done, we can leave whenever you want…or stay. Either way."

Fifi hadn't heard most of what he'd said. She was fixated on *emergency*.

"When did he leave? Did he say what the emergency was?"

"Oh, you literally just missed him. I'm surprised you didn't pass each other just now," Gabe said. "He said something about the cat, kittens, and emergency."

"Oh no!" Fifi kissed Gabe on the cheek and hollered over her shoulder before she left, "Thanks for the dances! I had a wonderful time catching up."

She ran out of the venue and straight to the parking lot. She heard the rumble of a truck and followed it until she saw headlights traveling down one row of cars over. When she jumped out in front of it, she put her hands out as if willing it to stop, then ran to the passenger side of the truck.

When she opened the door to hop in, Doc laid into her. "What the hell was that, Fifi? I could have hit you."

"Oh, you wouldn't have hit me. I had plenty of time to jump out of the way. What are you waiting for? Let's go."

"Go where?"

"To the emergency. Gabe told me. He said something about mama cat and her babies."

Doc floored it and tore out of the parking lot. "She's fine. I'm actually taking a page out of your book."

"Meaning?"

"Meaning we have a couple of baby raccoons meeting us at the barn, and they're tiny. They sound pretty fresh."

"Fresh?"

"Brand new," he said.

"And the mother?"

"She didn't make it, but they might."

"Wow. What is with this place and all the crazy animals?"

"It happens everywhere, but you probably just don't hear about it. Welcome to small-town mountain life." He laughed.

"So, what's from *my book*?" she asked.

"If a llama can care for a deer, maybe a nursing cat can nurse baby raccoons. You see stories like this everywhere, so why not here? Worst case, the team bottle-feeds round the clock for a while."

"It's a fantastic idea. Doc..." She paused. "It's going to work. I can feel it."

"Let's hope so. Night feedings are the worst." He laughed.

"It isn't Gabe."

"What isn't Gabe?" Doc asked as they pulled up to the barn.

"I found a letter. It was tucked under my purse at the table when I went to put out a minor fire at the lemonade station. Figurative, not a literal fire."

"Oh really?"

"Yeah. There's no way Gabe could have put it there because there wasn't a chance for him to do it without me seeing. Someone did it while we were dancing."

"Well, what did it say?"

"I don't know. I haven't read it yet. Everything happened so fast." Fifi followed Doc into the barn.

"Then read it. It's not like they've been long or involved," Doc poked fun.

"Fine."

Dear Fifi,

You're my favorite hello and hardest goodbye...stay?
Love, Santa

"Hmm... I don't know where to begin. You know what? If this is meant to be, whoever it is will stop me. They'll confront me. If this is real...I'm leaving it up to the universe. I'm still waiting for that big neon sign." She shrugged.

"You don't sound too disappointed it isn't Gabe. Did I miss something? He's all you talked about last night."

"Gabe is a really nice guy, but he isn't my type." Fifi shrugged. "Plus, he has a date over in Arrow Springs tomorrow. We spent the night catching up is all. Good news, though, I remember him now."

"Well, that's something. At least you got a friend out of the deal."

"Yeah, I suppose. But what does it matter now? I begged the universe for some sort of sign, and this is what it gave me. I'm back to square one. Looks like I'm leaving."

Doc took a minute to work on the baby raccoons and assess their health. Fifi watched as he and his tech went to great lengths to carefully introduce them to mama cat, taking their time to let *her* choose the babies. She sniffed them, inspected them, even licked one of them. Doc let her move closer to them without putting them in harm's way until she finally plopped down on her side so her kittens could nurse. When one of the raccoons searched her out, she didn't reject it.

They sat for more than an hour, watching nature take an interesting twist as the cat finally accepted the baby raccoons. It worked.

"It's like she knows they needed her," Fifi whispered.

"Maybe she does. Animals can be very intuitive and emotional. We just don't give them enough credit."

"So, what's next?" Fifi asked.

"We watch them, make sure they continue to bond and that she can sustain the extra mouths. At some point, we may have to help her out and bottle-feed, but this is the best thing for them right now. Mother Nature at her best."

"It's just lovely. This place. What you do," Fifi said, tears threatening. "What you do is important. These animals need you, and so do all the animals to come. You know there are groups in Holly-weird that eat this stuff up and would fundraise to save a rock or a street sign. I'll make some calls. These animals will be funded. I just know it."

"You'd do that? But you're leaving?" Doc questioned.

Fifi laid her head on his shoulder and watched the cat take in two orphan raccoons. "I am. But you don't have to."

"You said Holly-weird." Doc snorted.

"Yeah, well…perspective," Fifi said, pointing at the cat nursing the baby raccoons.

17

SUNDAY

IT WAS THE FINAL DAY OF THE FESTIVAL — THE TOWN'S Christmas breakfast together. Fifi rummaged around the house, getting ready in silence. The last day of the festival meant her time in McKenzie was almost up and she'd be heading back to LA. It was bittersweet. Though she had an entire life there, she wasn't sure it was the life she wanted anymore. She had options, but she didn't know which ones she was supposed to take.

There wasn't a letter, though it was still early in the day. She feared the one she'd received at the dance was the final one. What more could her Santa say? He was already telling her goodbye. He expected her to leave. That had to be what it meant — she wasn't meant to stay.

Fifi'd been up extra early so she could check on the animals and make sure they were all still doing well. She'd opted to leave Dallas in the barn because he seemed happier there on his log, and the heat was good for him. He didn't have to wear a sweater anymore like he did inside with the air conditioner running. Even he seemed to have fallen for this place. Sure, he was a sloth, but he seemed happy in McKenzie.

Fifi grabbed her things and went to meet Doc as they had each morning when they went to town.

"You ready to go?" she asked, catching up with him outside the barn.

"You go ahead without me. I'll meet you there."

"But the truck. You said I couldn't drive it."

Doc handed her the keys. "If I've learned anything about you in the past several weeks, it's that you can handle pretty much anything."

"Wow. Thank you. That means a lot coming from you." She tossed him a gentle elbow to the side. "Are you sure you don't want to go together? I can wait."

"No. I have a couple of house calls to make on my way in. I'll meet you there, though."

Fifi noticed something was off. He wasn't himself. His smile was forced, and he hadn't teased her or offered a single eye roll. "Is everything okay?"

"Yeah. Fine." He gave her another forced smile.

"Are…*we*…okay?" she questioned carefully, afraid they weren't and he was going to say so.

"Of course we are. Why do you ask?"

"Something just seems…off."

"Nope. I'm good. The animals are good. You're letting them stay. It doesn't get *much* better than that."

"Right," she said, noticing he didn't mention anything about her. "Oh, hey. I got an email this morning. I wasn't expecting it so soon, but my friend in LA…she loved my manuscript. Already sent it to her team in New York and wants to meet in the next week or so to discuss the details."

A genuine smile finally crossed his face. "That's fantastic,

Fifi. Your passion project was a success. So, what does that mean for you?"

"I don't know." She shrugged. "That's the problem. I still don't know."

Fifi looked at the keys in her hand. "Oh, you gave me the good truck. No manure two days in a row!"

Doc laughed. "The horse trailer is still hooked up to the other truck. When I said you can handle almost anything, I didn't mean towing a horse trailer."

"And there he is, folks. The real Doc Bain and all his snarkiness." She tossed the keys in the air and promptly caught them as she made her way to the truck to head to town.

FIFI FOUND HER NAME CARD AT THE CHRISTMAS BREAKFAST and took her seat. The seat next to her was reserved for Doc and still empty. It would be a shame if he got caught up with his patients and had to miss this. She'd never met a person so dedicated to what they did while doing it for next to nothing. His humility was unmatched, as was his generosity. He was a good man. One of the best. A total catch.

Fifi was shocked by that thought, unsure what made her mind drift in such a direction. He'd had his heart broken before and seemed content with his life with the animals, though. From the day she arrived, it was evident he was off-limits.

Too bad he wasn't her Santa. But that would be too easy. The idea of leaving McKenzie was starting to weigh on her, but she had nothing to stay for other than some man's misfit animals, and that wasn't enough. In fact, at this rate, maybe the Santa thing was a joke. How would she really know? Not a soul seemed to know a thing about those letters and a secret that big…in McKenzie? Well, that just didn't happen. The people here knew what she was having for breakfast before she even ate it most days…that's how little there was left to secret.

The buffet line had died down, and the crowd was starting to get louder as they each finished their meals. Fifi had no idea why she was still there. She wasn't feeling very social. Quite the opposite. Doc wasn't going to make it, and the last thing to unfold for this event was Santa stopping by one last time. Old man Tilly was always the last Santa. Fifi wasn't sure why; the man smelled of cheap whiskey and cigars most days.

She grabbed her purse and started to make her way to the exit when she heard Lou Shaw holler, "Santa's here, and he brought some friends! Everybody line up."

"Friends?" Fifi said quietly to herself. "I don't remember this being part of the plan. This ought to be interesting."

She leaned in the doorway and waited to catch a glimpse of Santa's mysterious friends. The side door opened to a booming, "*Ho, ho, ho,*" and in walked the man in question.

"Now, everyone be quiet. We don't want to scare Santa's special guests," Lou said. When the crowd didn't comply, she let out a high-pitched whistle to get everyone's attention. "Shut it, you hooligans. Santa's had a long night. Keep it down."

Fifi laughed. Classic Lou — no filter. Fifi took that as code for Santa had a little too much to drink the night before at the dance and wasn't ready for loud noises just yet, so she turned to leave. When the crowd hushed to barely-there *oohs* and *aahs*, she looked over her shoulder to see what the fuss was about.

A gasp escaped her, and tears filled her eyes. "It can't be."

Her eyes locked with Santa's, and he nodded in her direction, earning a soft giggle. Making her way through the crowd, she pushed all the way to the front of the line, where she was promptly scolded.

"Hey, lady. No cuts," a little boy said.

"Oh, excuse me. I'm very sorry," Fifi said, filing to the back to wait her turn.

Fifi laughed at the sight before her. How could she have missed this when it made the most sense of all? Each of the Santa letters played through her head, and she was able to see what she hadn't before. Every one of those notes pointed to one person, but he hadn't exactly made it obvious, throwing her off his trail. He'd pay for that.

She was thrilled as the line dwindled down to three, then two, then just one more kid. Leave it to the last one to be the neediest and chattiest.

"Hey, did you see they put out all the cookies and ice cream over there?" Lou said to the little girl. "Better get over there before those boys eat it all."

Without a second thought, the girl ran off without even a goodbye.

"Wow. Cookies are serious business around here." Fifi laughed. "I like your reindeer."

"I'll let you in on a secret. The big one is a llama. The antlers aren't real."

"You don't say?" Fifi chuckled. "And the little one?"

"Oh, she belongs to some fancy writer chick from Hollywood and her sloth. She's just a regular old mountain deer from McKenzie."

"Fancy, huh? She sounds awesome."

"She is," Doc said. "Little slow in the romance department, but…"

"I hear it's because the guy she lives with doesn't tell her things…like how he feels…"

"Touché," he said. "Maybe it's because she was looking for neon signs from the universe instead of what was right in front of her."

She nodded and mirrored the sentiment. "Touché."

"Is this neon sign big enough for you?"

"Why didn't you tell me you were a Santa? I would have known immediately."

"I'm not. I'm just a fill in for old man Tilly when he hits the bottle a little too much. It happens about every other year."

"He was your house call," she surmised.

"Every year, I stop by to pick him or the suit up. It's always a gamble."

"So, you brought Lucy and Jane Doe just in case?"

Doc shrugged. "He sat at the bar all night. I had a good feeling I was going to need these two."

"So, what's next, Doc?"

"I was just going to ask you the same thing."

"Well, I was thinking since I have a lot of writing to do now, or so it seems, and a bunch of animals — I think you said I have six — it might be easier if I just stay here to go through all my gram's stuff, and…you know, save animals."

"Are you sure about that?"

"I'm not sure of anything, but that's the best part, Doc."

"Will ya just kiss the girl? I got mistletoe and everything," Lou said, holding white flowers above them.

"Actually, that's lobelia, not mistletoe," Doc corrected.

"Okay, smart-ass. It's also July…so improvise."

Doc was lost in Fifi's gaze when he shrugged. "Yes, ma'am."

And he kissed her. It didn't matter who was watching, that the crowd was cheering, or that the children were all saying *ew*. He just kept kissing her. Without a single word, he told her everything she needed to know — the big neon sign asking her to stay.

Pulling away, he reached inside his red fur jacket and pulled out a red envelope. "This was my backup plan if Tilly showed up today. I was going to hand you this and hope it wasn't too late."

"Oh, Doc..." Fifi's eyes began to fill with emotion. "I don't think I would have been able to leave even if you hadn't. I think I belong here, and if I don't...too bad. You're stuck with me anyway."

DEAR FIFI,
We only regret the chances we didn't take...please stay?
Love, Santa

The End, For Now...

ABOUT STEPHANIE ST. KLAIRE

Stephanie St. Klaire is a Pacific Northwest native currently living in Portland, Oregon with her husband, five children, and two ferocious lap dogs that are used to the finer things in life like sleeping all day. When she isn't writing, she can usually be found with a plate full of taco's, a side of bean dip, and probably some gummy bears while being a little bit hippy and a lot bit busy mom'ing and wife'ing.

When she's not tossing around gritty crime show inspired serial killers and diabolical bad guys, she likes to make people pee their pants a little with a good romcom. Sometimes, her worlds collide, and she writes really funny stuff right before she kills people off on the pages! She loves murder and mayhem as much as a good laugh and HEA! That's why she's a die-hard Hallmark junky but loves her gritty crime shows – balance!

Stephanie has always been a storyteller, with the gift of "gab", and a life-long goal to be a writer. Unfortunate circumstances with her health, finally

afforded her the time to do so. Irony at its best, she began writing her first novel at an adverse time, to escape her circumstance and explore the stories in her imagination for relief. She is happy to share those stories with her readers, and bring a little fun, entertainment, and of course smexy characters to the pages.

Follow Stephanie St. Klaire on Social media to learn

more about her, how often she really eats taco's, and to keep up with her work.

*Get a **FREE** ebook when you sign up for SSK's non-spammy newsletter...*
www.stephaniestklaire.com/newsletter

Join Stephanie's private Facebook Group & Other Places to Find SSK:
www.stephaniestklaire.com/findssk

WHAT TO READ NEXT BY SSK

McKenzie Ridge Series

Rescued

Hidden

Forgotten

Fearless

Redemption

McKenzie Ridge Novellas

Christmas in July

Brother's Keeper Series

Declan (pt 1)

Declan (pt 2)

Liam

Luke

Dace

Wylie

Love, Cass (a series companion novel)

The Keeper's Series

Close Encounter (pt 1)

Close Encounter (pt 2)

Deadly Pursuit

Fatal Diversion

Royal Reckoning

Daddy Diaries

Volume 1

Faux-Mance Novels

Liar

Rumor Has It

Sneaking Around

Bed Buddies

FREE E-BOOK!

Read Book 1 in the McKenzie Ridge Series…FREE!!!

FREE E-BOOK!

Read Book 1 in the Brother's Keeper Series…FREE!!!

FREE E-BOOK!

Read Book 1 in the Brand New Keeper Series…FREE!!!

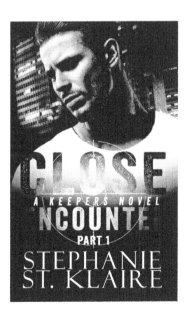

FREE SAMPLE - RESCUED
CHAPTER 1

Blood curdling screams, high pitched and ear piercing, were all she could hear. Sam felt intense confusion by her surroundings, not understanding where she was or where the sounds were coming from. What just happened, who was screaming, and why wouldn't it stop? Her body pulsed as sharp pain she couldn't identify flooded her from head to toe. It was so intense, it made her dizzy. She hurt everywhere. It hurt to move, to think even. The pressure in her head was nauseating.

Trying to formulate answers, she struggled to remember where she was. Her last recollection was being in her car. She remembered seeing something bright ahead. Although foggy, it was blinding. Then she heard that haunting scream. She needed to pull over. She shouldn't be driving — not like this — but she couldn't seem to do anything. Everything around her was so still.

It was dark, and everything was fuzzy. She writhed for clarity, attempting to overcome the confusion that left her in a groggy haze, sparking new hints of fear. A sense of heaviness weighted her chest like a cement slab, making it harder and harder to breath, each gasp becoming sharper and more shallow than the last. More lights surrounded her. The bright, blinding white light was replaced with changing colors flashing through the sky, surrounding her. There must have been an accident, but she couldn't see it. The screams were all she could remember. This had to be a dream.

Her world finally came into focus. Colton Sparks was standing to her left, and he was talking to her. Man, he was hot in his fire turnouts. She was indeed in her car, and he was standing next to her car. But what the hell was Colton saying? His look was so upsetting, so full of concern, so unlike Colton. She was struggling to hear him, to understand what was going on or how she could help. This was definitely a dream, Sam decided, because Morgan Jameson appeared as Colton stepped slightly farther down the car with a large object in his hand, some sort of tool. This was getting more confusing by the minute. Morgan shared a similar concerned expression as she began to speak. Morgan's mouth moved, but the words eluded Sam. She was probably asking her a plethora of questions. Always a cop, that one.

As Colton and Morgan backed away in a rush, Blake Cooper from the local PD and Jessie Clarke from Fire could be seen in the blurred distance, rushing around with a handful of others. Ah, the whole gang was here. It was a work dream. It had been a busy week, after all, so weird dreams were a given in her line of work, especially when she was sleep deprived. Sleep had eluded her the last several nights, thanks to a certain man who gave her goosebumps — the dreamy kind of goosebumps.

Sam couldn't say anything, and she no longer saw her friends by the car, just the lights fading in and out. Unsure where everyone had gone, she started to feel unsettled. She could hear the voices now, all around her. There was shouting, and what sounded like some sort of saw. None of this was making sense. A strange sensation fell over her. It wasn't a dizziness, but it wasn't still either. It made her feel funny. Her body began to feel light; it didn't seem to hurt anymore. She felt cold, although it was the middle of summer. If she didn't know any better, she would have thought she was floating. She heard voices again, including *his*.

She opened her eyes to find Dawson Tayler. Oh, she was definitely dreaming again, about the sexy EMT who flooded her thoughts by day and controlled her dreams by night. After last night's roll in the hay, or riverbank, she thought he was out of her system, or at least her dreams. Apparently not. She had to admit, it was a damn good roll, and she wouldn't mind a repeat.

* * *

It was another hot night in the bus. Dawson and his partner, Carigan, were dispatched to a single MVA on the dark, winding back roads tracing the outside of town. With lights and sirens blaring, they came upon the scene, finding Fire and PD already there — and it was bad. The car, or what was left of it, was wrapped around a big Ponderosa. It wasn't even recognizable, just a heap of metal and glass everywhere. Smoke was rising from what was likely the head of the car, billowing up the trunk of the tree.

"Jesus, Carigan, it looks like they need the morgue pickup, not an ambulance," Dawson said to his partner as they approached, seeing the full spectrum of what they had been called to. These calls were never easy. "Whoever is in there, God bless them for surviving so far. What a freaking mess. I hope we got here in time, Cari."

Having seen this before, especially during peak tourist

season, Carigan replied sympathetically, "Probably another drunken tourist from the rodeo, lost on the back roads."

As they jumped out of the ambulance and grabbed their equipment, Colton Sparks from Fire intercepted Dawson, stopping him before he could approach the victim. Dawson didn't like the look on Colton's face. Something was wrong. Watching over Colton's shoulder, eyeing the wreckage, a light, stealthy tingle drove through him as familiarity set in. He was piecing the demolished car back together in his mind when Colton dropped an earth-shattering bomb.

"Hey, Daws, hold up, man — you need to know. Shit... um, I'm sorry, but it's Sam. She's hurt real bad, man. Real bad." Colton placed his hand on Dawson's shoulder, full of sympathy and support for his friend. "You okay, man? You got this?"

Stunned, no words to be found, Dawson stared, watching as Jessie and the others from Fire peeled back sections of the car with their equipment. Sam was trapped in that pile of metal, and he was there to rescue her. He had just been with her last night, probably one of the best nights Dawson had ever had. He was at a loss over how his world had turned upside down so quickly. They were both on shift tonight, him on the ambulance, her in the ER, and they had promised to see each other — something Dawson had been looking forward to since leaving her the night before — but not like this — *never* like this.

Taking in the scene before him, Dawson felt the ground shift as the gravity of the situation fell heavy upon his shoulders. This wasn't just a wreck or a fender bender. There wasn't a word for the enormity of what sat right in front of him, wrapped around that tree. Smoke floated from the pile of wreckage, fluids spilled from all over, and blood appeared to be everywhere. Overwhelmed didn't begin to explain what he was feeling.

Then Dawson saw *her*. Pale, nearly gray, lifeless, covered in lesions and gashes, bruises already appearing, even in the darkness of the night. Her battered, injured body just lay there as her eyes blankly stared, mouth opening and closing, searching for sound, or maybe air. Without understanding, Dawson felt his heart crack in two as he watched this woman cling to life.

"Tayler, grab the cart, damn it! Get over here. She's ready for extraction! Let's go!" Carigan shouted to her partner, needing his assistance as she stabilized their patient for removal.

Shaken from his daze, Dawson grabbed the gurney and ran to assist his partner, setting aside his feelings for Sam and what had happened, looking at her strictly as his patient. They quickly, but carefully, removed her from the unrecognizable mound of shredded vehicle, the top peeled away like a tin can. He wouldn't let her die, not today, not on his watch. They wouldn't end this way.

* * *

Dawson was staring at her, his expression blanketed in concern and worry. Why was light-hearted Dawson looking so damn serious? Where was that panty-melting smile and charm? Sam looked around with her eyes only, unable to move her head. It was so bright and sterile-looking. Were they in his ambulance? Dawson grabbed something from above her and briefly fidgeted with her arm. She couldn't feel much, but she knew those were his hands — his touch was exhilarating and unmistakable. She felt him. She finally felt something that wasn't pain or numbness. He was holding her hand, and she could finally hear his words.

"Sam, please stay with me. You're going to be okay, baby. Hang on, okay?" Dawson said anxiety lacing his words. "Fight, honey. We're almost there. You're going to make it. You've got to fight!"

Be okay? Going to make it? Panic struck as reality set in. Something was wrong. Something *had* happened…to *her*. She couldn't feel anything other than his warm hand and the heaviness on her chest. Why couldn't she feel anything? Oh my God. It *had been* an accident, and she was the victim. They were all there for *her* — Colton, Morgan, Dawson — all the lights — something happened to her! Dawson squeezed her hand. He looked down, eyes pinched closed, and was talking again. What the — was he…*praying*?

Oh shit! Oh shit, this was bad, really fucking bad! Sam's last thought before everything got cold, dark, and silent…was Ellie.

* * *

Dawson was taken aback by the overwhelming emotions rushing in. He continued to talk to Sam while she drifted in and out of consciousness, finding himself on auto-pilot. While he assessed the deep longing and hurting in his chest, Dawson said all he could to comfort her, prayed even, as he took it all in.

Head to toe, covered in injuries, bleeding immensely, and frightened by the gash and swelling on her head, Dawson was relieved when they arrived at the emergency room and she was still alive. At the ready, the staff met them at the doors, emotions and fear evident, all anxious to receive their co-worker, their friend, sweet Sam, as their next patient.

"Cari, what do we have?" asked the thirty-something, highly accomplished, Doc Charles, an ER favorite and probably the best doctor to care for Sam.

"MVA, unconscious female, mid-twenties, BP 95/60 and dropping, multiple traumas to the…" Carigan rattled off, completely by the book, not letting emotions get involved, until her dear friend was handed over to those who would be charged with saving her. She could break down later, when Sam was in the right hands.

"Where's my other nurse? All hands on deck!" Doc hollered, scanning the staff surrounding the gurney, waiting for answers before examining the patient laying in front of him.

"You're looking at her, doctor. Our vic is Sam," replied a teary Nurse Jan, senior to her peers, deeply affected by the visual impact of Sam's injuries.

"Son of a… Let's go. Trauma one. Everything we've got, people!" choked Doc, realizing the extent of the injuries to tackle. The emotion of the situation concerning one of their own overcame him briefly before he led Sam away, ready to fight whatever battles her injuries presented.

With a blank stare, completely stunned, Dawson stood there, watching his colleagues wheel Sam off, not knowing if it was the last time he would see her. *God*, he hoped not. Not this, not again.

Dawson finished his shift in a daze. The rodeo was in town and that's where they'd spent most of the night. First, they tended to a call for a toddler with corn in his nose and his frantic mother. Toddlers with small objects shoved in various orifices were a pretty common call, even if it wasn't typically an emergency, but this kid managed to get what appeared to be half the cob up there. There were also a handful of bumps and bruises from the inevitable rowdy drunken cowboy brawls. The eye-roller of the evening, however, was a man passed out in the park, naked. Who gets that drunk? When the rodeo was in town, they saw all kinds of crazy, and tonight was no exception. For the first time ever, Dawson didn't love his job…he didn't want to be here.

* * *

Back at the hospital, Dawson found himself standing at the foot of Sam's bed. The black and blue covering every inch of her exposed skin was startling, leaving her nearly unrecognizable. The cuts to her head and face were equally shocking. Flashing back to the scene, he could only imagine what was beneath the bandages and splints that concealed the worst of her injuries. The sight of her damaged body moved him, an all too familiar emotion Dawson thought he buried a decade ago.

Despite her traumatic injuries, she looked peaceful, like she was only sleeping, but the sounds of the machines monitoring her, and ultimately keeping her alive, reminded him she was anything but at peace. What happened? What would cause such a dramatic and horrifying accident? It's the middle of summer, the roads are clear, and all the locals are very cautious of wildlife wandering in the road. It just didn't make sense why she hit that tree, that far off the road, that hard.

Everly Shaw, Sam's best friend and their colleague, walked in, catching him in deep thought. As a nurse on staff, Sam's emergency contact, and adoptive family, she was privy to Sam's lengthy list of injuries. Focused on Sam's face, still beautiful even if roughened, Evie began to share the outcome of Sam's accident.

He heard the words broken, punctured, fracture, and maybe even concussion, but he wasn't sure. Dawson was completely consumed by the desire to help her, see her healed. Everly's final words were loud and clear and shook him from the subject of his distraction. His heart stopped for a moment and the wind knocked from him when she said, "Coma."

Sam was in a coma. Evie rambled on for who knows how long, then he was alone again. Evie had slipped out without notice. It was only him and Sam. Dawson began to reconcile the feelings and emotions engrossing him. He didn't understand them. It had been years since he felt anything for anyone. Dawson fell asleep to the beeps and chirps, hearing every breath she took, in the chair next to her bed, holding her hand.

FREE SAMPLE - RESCUED
CHAPTER 2

Taylor and Tayler — it was the joke amongst their colleagues. Dawson Tayler, EMT. Sam Taylor, ER nurse. It never failed, when someone yelled out "Taylor" in their presence, they both answered, usually in unison. Since it was a small mountain town hospital, where everyone knew everyone, it was common for emergency medical, fire, and police to comingle, as well as the local ER staff. They all worked together often, were fast friends, and understood each other's worlds a little too well.

Nobody used their first names, since this kind of camaraderie was different. You either went by your last name or some sort of ridiculous nickname. The worst were those nicknames earned by stupid deeds or mistakes in the field. Once declared, they stuck forever, never to be lived down. This crowd was tight. They were there for each other, supported each other — they were family.

Sam and Dawson tended to spend their down time with the same characters from the hospital and the House — the station that housed all of Fire, EMS, and Police. All departments shared the same building and quarters, intermingling.

As unconventional as it may have been, it worked for their small tourist town cradled amongst the Cascade Mountains in Oregon. They were more efficient that way. They crossed lines and helped each other, allowing their small force to have a big impact.

Dawson and Sam both declared the single life as the only life, but sparks flew, and the heat was undeniable — obvious to everyone but Taylor and Tayler. Associates through work for years, they both struggled to ignore the curiosity surrounding one another, always trying to maintain those unfortunate professional boundaries that were bound to fail eventually, if only one of them would remove the invisible stick up their stubborn ass. They bantered, playing off their similar last names, and flirting shamelessly at work and outside of work when everyone ended a shift at The Pump House to decompress before calling it a night.

It never went any further, even though both thought about it…often. No, neither would take the next step. Neither one did the dating thing, and they most definitely didn't do *relationships.* The thought of either was like a quick, cold shower. No thank you. They were content with where things stood, completely safe, unattached, and single.

Taylor and Tayler, as silly a joke as it was, was their connection. Confusion over who was being summoned in the ER, or at The Pump House after a shift, generated as many laughs as it did opportunities to acknowledge each other. Dawson and Sam may have been able to avoid the obvious, but everyone around them saw it for what it was — they liked each other…a lot.

* * *

Dawson Tayler was a humble and modest man. Quiet even. As a child, he had a deep desire to help, starting with stray or injured animals, but ultimately being called to save his fellow man. His kindness and warm soul made him an outcast amongst his family. From a deep-rooted, ruthless, business-savvy family, Dawson was living an average life his family would have been appalled by…if they were alive. Although his heart was hardened and his soul numb, his instinct to help people remained.

A gentleman through and through, as his mama raised him to be, Dawson stood at over six feet tall, with sun-kissed skin and a chiseled body of rolling muscles. He had raven black hair, day old facial scruff, and the greenest, emerald eyes that made hearts break and panties melt. He was a bit of a man-whore when the opportunity presented itself, and present it was. Often. Dawson Tayler, a no strings, man's man had a stockpile of numbers to call at midnight, but not a soul to give him anything else. He liked it that way.

Regardless of his declaration for eternal bachelorhood, his satisfying life, emotionless as it was, began to change because of her. Dawson found Sam a mystery. He was drawn to her, wanted to figure her out, with or without clothes. It didn't help that she was *hot*. After many months of brazen flirting, he still knew very little about her, and he wanted to solve the mystery. Who was the real Sam Taylor, and why was she so damn captivating? Dawson wanted to ask her out. Not on a date — ask her out because he *didn't* date.

Sam Taylor, a storming ball of five-foot and a handful of inches fire, defined the word fighter. Her long, dark locks, slate blue eyes hooded with long, thick lashes, and full rosy lips harassed Dawson every night in his sleep. Her compact size was athletic in nature, complimented by perfect curves in all the right places — curves he wouldn't mind exploring.

She was so sexy, it should have been a sin, and he was a willing sinner.

Sam found herself living the life she'd always dreamed... sort of. With a flakey mother, divorced who knows how many times, Sam's childhood was as unremarkable as her name. Sam — not Samantha, not even Sammy — just Sam — that was as good as it got from the woman she referred to loosely as *mother*.

Her life was destined to be full of trials. Sam was practically raised by her best friend Everly's grandmother, Granny Lou. Although not ideal, Sam didn't regret one bit of her childhood. She always had big dreams to be a nurse, and so she was. She was a no-nonsense girl in life, and in the ER, doling out her fair share of snarkiness and rejection to doting men wanting to explore the hard ass that was Sam.

* * *

"Hey, Taylor, you off tomorrow?" he asked, followed by his knock-your-socks-off smile.

"Yep! You?" she replied, acting as though the mere conversation, let alone question, didn't faze her in the least or make her palms sweat.

"Sort of. I picked up a graveyard for Jack, so I'm not on until midnight." Dawson replied as he sat on the stool at the nurses' station.

"I heard Shelly was having the baby tomorrow!" she said with excitement for her friend, Shelly, Jack's wife. "Poor girl. She's what, like two weeks overdue?"

"Yes, something like that." Not interested in discussing children or where they came from, he replied with a dose of disinterest before finishing his thought. "We're all chipping in and covering shifts for him so he doesn't have to use up all his vacation time before the kid even gets here."

"Baby," Sam corrected, with an eye-roll for the Neanderthal-like reference to the little bundle.

Smiling, with raised eyebrows, Dawson tossed her an ounce of sarcasm, "Yes, *honey*?" he deadpanned, proud of himself for the clever reply.

Clearly not impressed or charmed by his wit, on the outside anyway, she amended her previous thought, replacing the prior eye-roll with a shake of her head. "Baby, Dawson. It's a baby, not a *kid*." On the inside, she was praying Dawson would leave before he made her sweat through her scrubs.

"Oh, gotcha, *honey*." Dawson was on a roll, getting under her skin, enjoying how uncomfortable he was making her, and he took that as a sign. It was almost as promising as that little bead of sweat accumulating between her brows.

"Don't you have somewhere to be, lives to save, ladies to charm?" she tossed out, trying to get rid of him before she showed all her cards.

He left his perch and began to follow her down the hall, her arms full of files, distributing each to its rightful place as she went. "Nope, only you. Is it working?"

"I don't need saving, and I'm immune to that hunky, I'm-too-good-looking-for-my-own-good charm." She squinted and immediately regretted her choice words. Crap, she just showed him her hand. So much for the poker face.

"So, you think I'm too good looking and hunky?" He upped the ante by tossing her a wink, topped with wiggling eyebrows and a sexy grin that revealed his adorable dimples — hook, line, and sinker.

"Get out of here, Tayler!" she said, putting her hand on his chest — his mighty hard, chiseled chest — and giving him a shove. Of course, he flexed the giant peck under her hand, sending a slicing tingle straight to her core, making her jump and pull back like it stung.

"Okay, I'm going, but first I wanted to let you know I'm taking you to dinner tomorrow." Not a question, a statement. No yes or no required, just an, *"Okay, see ya then."*

Her heart stopped, her face felt hot, and her palms began to drip sweat. Holy shit! Dawson had asked her out. Sam stood there wide-eyed, and damn it, she was actually thinking about it! What the hell! Her brain was saying, *"Run, you don't date!"* But those gorgeous green eyes and that sexy grin attached to that strong jaw were telling Sam and her lady parts to say, *"Yes, oh yes, please."* Oh my God, Dawson licked his lips while his gaze drifted to hers. Why was this turning her on? Why was *he* turning her on?

"I don't date, Dawson," she said, readying to walk away. "Especially co-workers and guys who change women as often as they change their underwear." The last part was punctuated with a sassy grin, proud of the below-the-belt hit. She finished him off with her own devilish side-eye and wink.

"I don't date either, and I'm not some kind of gigolo, Sam," Dawson struck back, a little offended. He may see the occasional nighttime visitor, but he wasn't what she was implying. Why did it bother him that she thought that about him? "I only want to have dinner with a friend and figure out what makes her...*her.*"

"Not interested. Not going to happen. It's dinner. It's a date. I don't need *figuring out.* I'm out!" Walking away again, moving to her next task, she quickly closed her eyes and took a deep breath. Dawson was having an effect on her she couldn't explain. It was pissing her off, or was it?

Giving her his best pitch yet, Dawson delivered a pretty convincing plea as to why this wasn't a date, but he was starting to wonder if maybe it was. "It's not a date. If it were a date, I would bring flowers, candy, and all that fluffy shit you girls like. I'm simply buying a friend dinner. We both have to eat, so why not together?"

"Drinks? Will there be dessert?" she questioned.

"Now you're talkin'. I can *do* dessert, whatever you want, wherever you want…"

"I meant like cheesecake or bread pudding, you ass."

"I know, I know, I'm only kidding." Dawson was excited he was wearing Sam down. He knew she would see it his way and meet him for this *non-date* date. "I figure if I start with the bar that high, you'll give in when I say, 'Cheesecake sounds amazing.'"

"Cheesecake is a date." Sam wasn't giving in. Dawson was tempting, but that was the problem.

"Fine, no cheesecake. Solely dinner, maybe a drink, friends, very public, not a date."

"Drinks…date."

"Fine, no drinks." Christ, Sam had rules, but he liked it. Dawson was enjoying the challenge. He clearly had her in final negotiations. Tomorrow night was looking good.

Sam paused as she assessed the situation, assessed *him,* her dark, hooded eyes and open mouth leaving her ponderings less than a mystery. She had a strict no dating rule, and was pretty confident that rule applied to smexy, sex-on-a-stick, co-workers especially. Nothing good would come from a Tayler and Taylor rendezvous — nothing good at all. Oh, who the hell was she kidding?

No matter how loud her instincts protested the idea of fraternization, her libidinous drive sat on her right shoulder, like the devil himself, whispering indecent lust-filled notions that were much more convincing than her good-intentioned constitutions. She turned a deaf ear to logic and reason, and fell victim to all the pheromones, or hormones, or whatever it was pushing her down the perilous path that was Dawson Tayler. She might have regretted this at some point, but she was certain it would be worth the thorny ride — or maybe it was a *horny* ride that would inevitably present itself.

She turned to him, looked him straight in the eye, and delivered her matter of fact terms. "No dinner. Breakfast. Baker's, after shift. Coffee and a fritter, very public, friends. I'll meet you there, *not* a date."

"Sold. See you at Baker's, *honey*," he said before kissing the back of her hand and walking away. And watch him walk away, she did. It was a glorious sight. That ass, those pants, and God help her, he was flexing his enormous biceps, giving her an intentional show. Smug son of a bitch.

With a wicked grin and a sexy wink that said anything but *just breakfast*, Dawson was gone. What the heck happened? How the hell had he done that? And why was she already wondering if it was appropriate to have first date nookie? Or after breakfast nookie, in this case. Maybe it was because Sam wanted to know if Dawson was really built the way she imagined him to be.

Her better judgment scolded her as she questioned her sanity — or lack thereof. *Geez, get it together, Sam*. She was humming at the thought of him, and those thoughts were naked and dirty. Why did Dawson have this effect on her? He wasn't the first hotter than hell guy to cross her path over the past few years. The House was full of them.

What was it about Dawson Tayler that made her think all men were bad but him? She couldn't answer those questions, but she was sure looking forward to figuring them all out, even the naked ones, over coffee and a fritter…maybe not in that order.

* * *

McKenzie Ridge was full of rustic mountain charm. Being in the Pacific Northwest, it appealed to tourists all year, with its ever-changing seasons and activities that surrounded their town. Main Street rested in the heart of town, both sides flanked with a variety of shops and eateries. Baker's sat on the edge of town, on the west side of Main Street, opposite the hospital that resided to the east.

Jed Baker, third generation owner, was about the best baker there was, especially when it came to his morning delectables. Baker's wasn't small, nor big, with its eclectic design. It was comfortable and accommodated its patrons reasonably as the morning hot spot amongst locals and even a few foodie tourists who saw him on one of those travel Food Network shows. It was a great place to meet…busy, lots of people — *not a date!*

Dawson arrived first, and found he was surprisingly nervous. Getting Sam here had been a contest he'd almost lost. Now, how did he keep her here? He wasn't sure what they were doing, other than *not dating*. Dawson wasn't even entirely sure why this was so important to him. What was it about Sam that had him so enamored, ready to break all his own rules? He was anxious to find out.

Not sure what she took in her coffee, Dawson ordered her a tall black and had all the add-ins at the table so she could dress it up herself. He figured an apple fritter was a safe bet since it was her idea, and because there wasn't a person around who didn't love those fresh morning fritters. Hoping his charm was enough to entice her to let her guard down, Dawson was only sure of one thing — by noon, the whole town would know they had been at Baker's *together*. Small town living at its best.

* * *

Sam had sworn off men her last year of college, and with good reason. Men were a liability. They weren't reliable, good for only a quick romp, some quicker than others, with no guarantee for that happy ending. Her problem was her lady parts disagreed with her every time she saw Dawson Tayler's larger than life frame, emerald green eyes, dark hair, and heaven sent physique.

He was quiet, reserved even, except with her. He was gentle and kind, maybe a little cocky at times, but in an endearing, maybe a tad bit charming way. Dawson Tayler could get a girl pregnant simply by looking at her. He was the epitome of sex, and anything with a pulse could see it. The look Dawson had in his eyes every time she glanced at him sent a shiver up her spine and a zing to her core.

Sam often wondered what a night in the sack with Captain Sexy Pants would be like, and then reality would hit her like an ice-cold shower. Dawson was tempting, oh so tempting. There was a story there — a tall, sexy story that made her throb in all the right places. Or maybe they were the wrong places, and she was just a horny old maid. She could never go out with him — he was far too dangerous — which was why this wasn't a "date."

FREE SAMPLE - RESCUED
CHAPTER 3

He watched Sam pull into a parking space across the parking lot where she sat for several minutes. Oh, to be a fly on that dash. As she got out, she paused, looked up, and shook her head, as if reconsidering her decision to be there. Dawson smiled as she shook it off and gave herself what looked like a pep talk. *That's right. Go get 'em, tiger.* It took her several minutes for her to find her way into Baker's.

She was easy on the eyes, and made him sweat with one look, even in those scrubs she was still wearing, but there was more there. Temptation was getting the best of him. Dawson had to figure out what it was about this little sex kitten that made him want her for more than a midnight run of naked Olympics. He knew she would push all the right buttons in bed, keeping him warm while he kept her satisfied — Dawson knew he was a scholar in the sack.

He imagined her sprawled across his sheets, crying out from his touch, pretty much every night in his dreams. They would please each other in bed, no doubt, but he wanted to please her in other ways too. He didn't know why, and he didn't like it. Dawson was better off alone. It made more sense that way…much safer.

His temptress was getting to him. For some reason, he was willing to take risks he had sworn off a decade ago. He needed to know why she invaded his sleep, confused his thoughts, and what made her Sam — *his* Sam.

* * *

"Hey, Tayler," she said, taking the bench across the booth from him.

"I ordered your coffee and fritter," Dawson proudly proclaimed, hoping that impressed her.

"What if I don't like coffee and fritters?" she questioned with a coy smile, challenging him, reluctant to make this easy for him.

"Then you probably shouldn't have said, '*Baker's, coffee and fritters.*'" Dawson quoted her words in a high-pitched retort, and an amused, you-aren't-fooling-anyone look.

"Touché, Tayler. Touché. And I don't sound like that." She was annoyed by his mocking, didn't like the stuffy snob he portrayed.

"You kind of do." He winked, busying himself with a packet of sugar for his coffee. "I didn't add anything to the coffee, but grabbed a little of everything."

"Oh, I like it just like this — tall, bold, and hot." As soon as she said it, she wished she could call it back. She had offered that one up to him on a silver platter.

"Are you still talking about the coffee or…" He left the *or* open-ended. He would let her fill in the blank and enjoy watching her squirm.

"Nice try. So, let's cut the crap. Why breakfast?" Her

quick change in direction didn't help her case. This was a one-time deal, and she wanted to make that clear.

"Breakfast was your idea. I wanted dinner."

"Okay, why this?" She flailed her arms around in a circle, indicating *this* meant *them*.

"Why not? We're friends. What's wrong with friends getting together for a bite to eat and getting to know each other better? We've worked together for a long time and know nothing about each other. Maybe I want to know Sam, the girl in the bakery, as well as Sam, the life-saving nurse." He made his point, delivering it with innocence. Friends… that's all this was.

"Interesting. We can play it that way. So, where are you from? What brought you to McKenzie Ridge to play super, hunky hero who saves lives?" She bit her tongue a second too late. She really needed to quit offering him her thoughts so easily — *hunky?* Really? *Shoot me now*, she thought.

"Super hunky? Okay, I can work with that. Well, about ten years ago, my entire family died in a plane crash. I was the only one left, so I *left*. I was supposed to be on that plane." He paused briefly, questioning how much was too much, before continuing. "I traveled a bit, but nothing felt like home except McKenzie Ridge. I grew up coming to this area. My uncle had a cabin not far from here. He would bring in all the cousins, and we would spend a few weeks together every summer," Dawson shared in a less than tactful way, not intentionally delivering a shocking admission.

"I had no idea, Dawson. I'm sorry. That must've been awful. What am I saying? Of course it was awful. I didn't mean to…" She was shocked and at a loss for words, which didn't happen often.

"Don't worry about it. You couldn't have known, and it was a long time ago. Isn't this why we're here? To get to know each other? Your turn. Spill it." He wasn't sure why he was sharing this, but the words just fell out, displaying his past like clothes on the line.

"Spill it? Oh, yes…well, I grew up kind of all over. My dad left before I was one, and my mom doesn't do single or broke, so we followed several *stepdads* around before landing here. That's when I met Evie and Granny Lou. They became my family. The rest is history." Simple and to the point, that was the short and sweet of it — and all she felt like sharing. It wasn't exactly a warm and fuzzy story in its entirety.

"What about your mom?" Confused by her admission, he briefly paused before questioning the obvious. There wasn't anyone else he knew of living in the Taylor or Shaw household. Where was the rest of her family?

"What about her? She's out there somewhere, married or chasing — gotta be around husband nine or ten…not sure." With years of practice under her belt, she was good at saying that with a straight face, and she had finally convinced herself it didn't bother her. "Once we were here, she trusted Gran, so she would go on 'trips,' and I would stay with Gran and Evie. Eventually, her *trips* became longer and more often, so she gave Gran guardianship, and that was that."

"She just left you?" Wincing at his own question, he realized natural curiosity reared its head and got ahead of him. Dawson didn't mean to ask such a pointed question, but he was genuinely shocked by her story. How does a mother leave like that?

"Well, no…yes…I don't know. It was better that way. I got Gran and Ev and got to go to the same school every year, have roots. It worked out for me." She honestly felt that way. They were family, more so than her mother or countless stepdads. "I couldn't imagine how my life would have turned out if I'd stayed with her, chasing man after man — what kind of life is that for a kid? Who even does that? *Bette Morrison*, serial bride and man chaser."

"Wow, that's…I don't even know what that is. Let's move on to something else. What do you like to do when you aren't at the hospital playing super seductive nurse and saving lives?"

That earned him a spirited laugh, one that was deep and spontaneous. He liked that, and hoped he saw more of *that* Sam. The morning continued as they shared simplicities in a light, non-date manner, like their hobbies, favorite foods, and several other nonsensical things that ended a very nice and enjoyable breakfast together.

* * *

Granny Lou spread gossip like wildfire, but only the good kind if you asked her. Mornings at Baker's were like a game of telephone. By the time the morning rush ended, juicy gossip got a whole lot juicier…steamy even. She knew a couple when she saw it, and Sam and Dawson were a mighty handsome one. They would make beautiful babies, in her wise, old, never-wrong opinion.

Granny Lou was a real kick in the pants. The old lady lacked a filter, but at least she was always honest. If you didn't like what you heard, it was probably because you needed to do some soul searching. Wisdom spewed as fluidly as sarcasm. There wasn't a person around who didn't love this lady. Her ears occasionally strayed into other people's business, and she was known to share stories — gossip — but her heart was always in the right place. Gardening, horses, matchmaking, and saving lost souls were her hobbies.

Granny Lou lost her husband twenty years ago and she'd never remarried, didn't even date really. She believed in only one true love, and she'd already had that. Tragedy followed again, only a few short years later, when her only son and daughter-in-law were lost in an accident. As the only living relative, willing and able, Gran took in her granddaughter, Everly, and they saved each other.

Everly was part of a packaged deal. Her best friend, Sam, came with her…most of the time. Sam's mother was more interested in men than her own daughter, leaving at any given moment to chase her true love: money. Granny loved that child like her own and preferred to have her around. She didn't trust the life her mama was providing, so there they were, a family.

Dawson and Sam hadn't even seen her when she'd stopped in for a caffeine fix to chase the doughy, sugar fix she ordered to go, but Granny sure saw them, and she was happy at what she saw. Sam was going to be harder to sell, but Lou saw something brewing, whether the two of them wanted it or not. Fate never got it wrong, and neither did Louise Shaw.

She just needed to draw it out for them, give them a road map of sorts. She didn't know Dawson's story — nobody did really — but she knew Sam's, and her gut told her Dawson was a good boy with a lost soul — nothing a little love couldn't fix. This was going to be her biggest triumph yet, and she was already patting herself on the back and high-fiving herself.

That was the benefit and burden of living in a small town — everyone knew everyone, and *everyone* knew *everything*. It was a foregone conclusion. Half the town was already buzzing about Taylor and Tayler, and bets were probably waging on the unlikely twosome.

* * *

As expected, Taylor and Tayler were the main topic of conversation around the hospital and the House. Both found themselves defending their new routine morning breakfasts as simply that: two people who need to eat before ending their day and starting over. The gang at the House was a little less forgiving, taking every opportunity they could to rub in the fact that Dawson was dating.

"Seriously, bro, you guys have been at Baker's every morning for weeks. That's dating. Getting any *perks*? I bet she's full of..." Colton started the ribbing. He *was* a relationship guy — or wanted to be, anyway.

"Shut it, Sparks. They aren't dates. You have breakfast *and* dinner with Blake here all the time. You two dating, man?" Dawson knew he was being overly sensitive, but protecting whatever it was he had with Sam felt instinctive — it was off limits, even to the people who knew them best. "Do you get burns from his scruff? I bet you like a good beard burn."

"Go to hell, Tayler! This is between you and Sparks. Besides, he's not my type." Blake Cooper could take a joke, and dish a few good ones himself, but giving beard burns to Sparks wasn't funny. He'd rather it be a five-foot-nothin' spitfire, but it simply wasn't in the cards for now.

"What do you mean, I'm not your type?" Sparks shot back. "Have you seen alllll this? You wish I played for the same team."

"Neither of you is worth a hissy fit. Get over yourselves." Jessie was a good sport, but boy, banter annoyed the crap out of her, and this was a shut-the-eff-up moment. Sometimes, she was better at being *one of the guys* than the guys, which was her way of surviving in a man's trade, all five-foot-three-inches of her. "If Tayler says they aren't dating, then they aren't dating. Some people are just casual that way, friends with *benefits*, if ya know what I mean."

"Of course you had to go there. Thought you were offering support from the female regime, but I guess you left all your estrogen at home." Appreciating her input, crass as it was, crap from Jessie was a compliment, and Dawson welcomed it.

"Suck it, Dawson, like seriously hard." A classic Jessie Clarke response — vulgar.

"Spoken like a true lady. Look, Daws, it's no one's business what you are doing. She's a nice girl. Who wouldn't get *buns* every morning if they could?"

"And there it is. I expected more from you, Morgan. And it's fritters. We eat fritters."

"All right, lay off, guys. You're all just jealous Tayler has someone to have breakfast with and none of you do," Carigan interjected, always kind, always level headed. Although around the same age, Carigan O'Reilly was the mother of the bunch, always making sure everyone was okay. "Daws, I do want to point out, as your partner and the person you spend most of your time with, you do seem to be a lot happier these days. I hear she's getting the same crap over at the ER, and survey says she's been smiling non-stop for weeks now. Non-dating looks good on you."

"Thanks for having my back, O'Reilly. So, I make her smile? Huh. Interesting."

Dawson could always count on Carigan to have his back, which was why they worked so well together. They watched out for each other, understood each other. He knew the gang was only giving him crap — they were his family, and that was what families did. Dawson would partake if it were any of them, but Sam was off limits to even them. They weren't dating, but they were certainly more than just colleagues, and something about that was both exciting and frightening.

It had been several weeks of mornings at Baker's. It wasn't even a question anymore, simply a *see you there* standing arrangement. They even found themselves there together, on a couple days off, not breaking routine. Dawson was really enjoying Sam, getting to know her, spending time with her. It was like they were old friends rather than new friends. He didn't know what this was or where it was going, but he really liked it…even if it was kind of like dating.

Today was much different, though. Their routine had been challenged, and Sam didn't like it. Dawson was one of the only EMTs who wasn't attached, didn't have family or consistent outside commitments to speak of, so he picked up a lot of extra shifts to cover for those who needed time off. Dawson wasn't going to be at Baker's because he was picking up a few extra hours to help out one of the guys at the House.

The sexual tension had been building. Far too many times, they had found themselves in precarious situations, nearly in the throes of passion before one of them broke the spell, remembering where they were just in time. Having public *get-togethers* was their saving grace since neither was much of an exhibitionist. Privacy would certainly lead to one thing, so they would keep things very public…for now.

Sam craved their daily custom. The idea of not seeing Dawson for breakfast left her with an unfamiliar and unwelcome sense of melancholy. She had the day off — her schedule was fairly open — so she suggested they meet for lunch at the pavilion in the park since she would already be over that way. It was the perfect solution, even if the fact that she *needed* a solution concerned her.

The park was large, several acres, surrounded by the beauty that was McKenzie Ridge — nature, views of the surrounding mountains, and of course, lots of people. The pavilion was nestled at the far end of the park, near the local equestrian center, Sugar Pine Stables, which bordered the east side. Not only could you rent rafts, canoes, and inner tubes to take down the creek, as well as rods and bait to fish, but you could also find some of the best hoagies and fried anything in town.

Dawson was elated by her desire to take this non-dating breakfast in a new direction, even if he was somewhat surprised. After all this time, and no matter how much she seemed to enjoy their non-dates, she was still pretty guarded with him. He would work on that, but this was progress, even if only slightly. Something in her past really made a mark on her. Dawson briefly thought it was the mother who kept leaving her, but something said there was more to this elusive event that erected walls around Sam. What was she protecting herself from?

It was a beautiful midsummer day, with clear blue skies and a gentle breeze to keep the day's heat at bay. The park was alive with people and nature alike, along with mind-blowing views of the surrounding mountain peaks and landscapes — the perfect non-date spot. They ordered their food and found a nice table under a large, shady tree, picking up where they'd left off from their last non-date. The squirrels and birds provided the entertainment, fighting over the food they scavenged for, keeping the afternoon light and easy.

"So, what brought you to the park today anyway? You mentioned you would already be over this way," Dawson prodded, curious to find out the real reason they were there for lunch rather than their typical morning meeting.

"Oh, I was next door at Sugar Pine Stables. I'm there every week."

"Every week? You ride?"

"Of course I *can* ride, but that's not why I go." She shifted in her seat, regretting her reply. She didn't have a good answer as to why she was really there if not to ride.

Dawson sensed some kind of unease and hesitation coming from her, like a secret spilled before she could catch it. She promptly tried to reel it in and deflect whatever it was she thought she'd just divulged. What was there to be uncomfortable about, with going to Sugar Pine Stables every week? It's an equestrian center, lots of people like horses and even volunteer. Perhaps this was part of the wall she had built around her. It was too personal, and she was letting him in faster than she was content with.

"You volunteer?"

"No…well, not really. I'm friends with Rene, who runs it, and Morgan Jameson goes often. Everly does too, for Search and Rescue stuff. I guess it just kind of rubbed off — something we all have in common," Sam replied, satisfied with her answer.

"Oh, I forgot they had a new person over there. Rene, that's right. She is so familiar to me, but I can't put my finger on it." Dawson's mind wandered, recalling seeing Rene Garcia at Sugar Pine and how oddly familiar she seemed, but the feeling must not have been mutual because she never gave any indication she already knew him.

"I thought that about Rene too! So familiar! She must have one of those faces because she isn't from around here." Sam recalled her first meeting with Rene. It was like running into an old friend from junior high — a serious case of déjà vu.

"Maybe we can go riding sometime. Have you ever been up the trails along the creek to the peaks? It's a pack-your-lunch-and-ride-all-day kind of adventure." Innuendo delivered, Dawson gave her a wink and left it at that.

"I haven't been up to the peaks. That might be fun," she countered, making it clear his message was received and quickly shot down. "How was your fried mushrooms and spicy mustard sour dog sausage thing?" she chuckled.

The awkward change of subject, and distracting laughter over his peculiar food combination, wasn't lost on him. She really wasn't comfortable talking about Sugar Pine and what it was to her. He would have to explore that. What was so secretive about the horses, or was it something about the stables? The more she became a mystery, the more intrigued he became.

"It's a beer brat, spicy mustard and sauerkraut, and it was delicious. My dad used to say, 'That'll put hair on your chest.' Try one next time!" he said, beating his chest with a closed fist.

A stunned look of familiarity crossed her face at his statement, but was gone as quickly as it came. Interesting. He was missing a piece of this puzzle — a big piece. Dawson didn't like secrets, but until he could whittle away at that wall of hers some more, it would have to be explored another day.

"Good. It smelled awful. I'll stick to hoagies, corndogs, and curly fries with lots of ranch dressing — the good stuff — but thanks! You ready to head out?"

* * *

Always a gentleman, he gathered their empty trays and wrappers and disposed of them while she waited next to the table. Dawson had grabbed her hand at some point as they walked to the parking lot to part ways and say goodbye. She let him hold it as if it was the most natural thing in the world and completely part of their non-dating routine. The more her mind sent up red flags and warnings, the more her heart reached for her guy. *Her guy*. She didn't know when he became her guy or all it entailed, but she had conceded and decided to live in the moment.

It felt good. *He* felt good. Sam didn't know what possessed her to suggest they break routine and meet for lunch. Their shifts had crossed that day rather than being on par with each other. But the idea of breaking their morning routine at Baker's and not seeing him for the day had disappointed her. Before she could stop herself, she had asked Dawson to meet her for lunch in the Pavilion at the park.

It still wasn't a date. No, she didn't date, but a lunch companion is always nice. Sam liked Dawson in a friends-who-have-coffee-after-work-every-single-day-and-lunch-when-breakfast-isn't-in-the-schedule kind of way. Friends held hands, and she liked how his big calloused hand felt wrapped around hers. She wondered where they would feel elsewhere.

That was all she was capable of having with a man — it was all she had room for and all she was willing to let in. Friends. He was something to be looked at, there was no question there, and what every good author wanted on the cover of their sexy books. Dawson was sex — the kind that sells! A lot! So she would stick to having a really smoking hot, sexy friend.

Sam found Dawson was more than just inspiration when she broke out her battery-operated best friend. There was much more to this man. The real Dawson was showing his true colors more and more, and she was enjoying him. It wasn't only those rippling muscles hiding beneath those t-shirts of his, or how amazing his ass looked in those navy cargo pants he wore for work, or how they squeezed his thighs, that made her burn and have to sit sideways, sending her mind straight to the gutter where she could hang out for days.

She wanted to squeeze his ass and a few other things. How he didn't burn a smoldering hole through the seat of his pants was beyond her. Speaking of ass and thighs, he would fit well between her own. What on earth was she doing, fantasizing in the middle of a busy family friendly park, holding Mr. Hot Pants' hand while picturing him between her thighs? She needed to get a grip — or a really cold glass of ice water to dump in her lap. There was more to Dawson. Sure, Dawson made her tingle everywhere, but he gave her sweet butterflies too.

Dawson wasn't a commitment guy. The only commitment he made was to keep his late night callers private. He hadn't had any late night company since that first morning at Baker's with Sam. Dawson was a virile man with manly needs, but he just couldn't seem to find interest anywhere but with Sam. It felt wrong to even consider a midnight romp with anyone else, like he was betraying something between them. This was new territory for him — territory he vowed to never explore again a decade ago. Your heart can't break if it isn't invested anywhere, but his heart had forgotten all the rules. So he made a temporary deal with himself to merely live in the moment...to see where this goes.

Dawson wanted more from her, to *know* Sam, not only her body, but *her*, to figure her out. Where did that sass and hard exterior come from? What happened to her to make her so invigorating, yet guarded? Dawson didn't understand his new desire. She was a menace with his emotions. He liked who he was around Sam. She drudged up old feelings and new ones Dawson didn't yet understand. He enjoyed how easy she was to be around.

Conversations were easy, and she wasn't impressed by all that charm Dawson laid on. Sam didn't buy it for a second, which he liked. He could simply be him, and she wanted nothing more *or* less. She was starting to find him just as interesting as he found her. She had actually invited him to lunch today, and it was Sam who had determined their mornings at Baker's were a regular thing rather than the occasional *only if there's time*. The more Dawson got from her, the more he wanted, and the more he looked forward to having.

A date. He was going to do it, the unthinkable — Dawson was going to ask her on a real date. Not a cup of coffee and apple fritter with half the town, or corn dogs in the park with the squirrels where they would talk about a mysterious horse hobby, but a real date. Dawson was consistent with his convictions, but this felt right, even if it did break all his rules. And he was willing to continue bending those rules to get more of her.

* * *

They approached her car when he turned her around so she was facing him, both arms on either side of her, so close, he could smell the sugary sweetness of cream from her dessert on her breath. So many times, they had found themselves in close proximity, within total make-out-in-front-of-everyone range, but one of them always pulled back. They were currently hand-holding friends, but they certainly weren't kissing friends. Until now, as far as he was concerned. Today, he was changing that rule too.

Trapped between two enormous biceps, wedged between her car and rock hard abs, with the deepest, wicked, green eyes locked on hers, she began to sweat. Panic set in. This was too intimate and way too public. She was surrounded by his massiveness and felt safe in his almost embrace. This man was overwhelming in every good sense of the word. Her faith in what was coming next outweighed her fear, and she stared back, inviting his next move.

She was overwhelmed by the scent that would forever be burned into her memory as Dawson — spicy yet earthy, masculine but sexy, and entirely way too hot. Unable to look anywhere but his eyes, she read his every thought as they darkened, and desire was the only thing readable. Anxiety was replaced by dirty thoughts of pressing her chest against his, tempting him, seeing what his response would be, and exploring that cocky mouth of his that held a scandalous grin. Shocked by her own thoughts, she blushed as he laughed, as if he knew what obscene things were going through her sinful mind.

Without even asking the question, Dawson took her response to his proximity as a yes and kissed her — long, deep, and hard. Her lips were soft, her mouth hot. He could have done this forever. She softened and leaned into him, hands straight to the back of his head. Oh yeah, he had read her just right. She was into him, and completely into this kiss. Where red flags and alarms would have been going off once upon a time, all he heard now was angels singing *hallelujah*.

One arm dropped as his large hand found her waist and paused slightly before moving south and resting his palm on her ass, pulling her closer so she could feel exactly what she was doing to him. She was overwhelmed by sensations she couldn't remember ever feeling. She was warm head to toe, and her body was buzzing, but more so than that, her heart was dancing. Jesus, he was good at this, and probably better at the other things that were racing through her head. Crap! What was she doing? They were in the middle of a parking lot, giving a really hot show to anyone interested! She would have to wave a "you're welcome" to the fan club when they were done.

Reluctantly, she broke the kiss and slowly pulled back from the pleasure he gave her and comfort she felt in his arms.

"Is that a yes?" he asked, still holding her close, his forehead to hers.

"Is what a yes?" She was confused, not sure where her legs went or how she was still standing.

"Tomorrow night. Seven o'clock. I'll pick you up." He stood tall, his hands around her waist. She wasn't getting out of here until she gave him the answer he wanted.

"Is that what that was? You asking me out? Wow, things really have changed!" She gave him a puzzled look, clearly stalling as the tug of war between her heart and mind ensued.

"No, that was a kiss, a really effing great kiss," he declared before his confidence softened and his tone changed to light and sweet, and perhaps a little insecure, afraid of receiving the wrong answer. "This is me asking you out. Would you like to go out tomorrow night? We're both off. It's like fate or something." He was really selling this, calling on fate for help. He sincerely wanted a date with this woman.

"But…we don't date." She was still stalling, wanting desperately to say yes, but lacking the courage. Every instinct in her body said absolutely not, but somewhere deep down in the depths of her soul, she was screaming, *"Hell yes!"*

"I know we don't. If you would rather stick to fritters at

Baker's, we can do that too, it's just not as fun." He lightened the mood, adding a little silliness, sensing how serious this had become for her, hoping to make this an easier answer.

"I love fritters…"

He kissed her again, interrupting her protest, but this time, it was the kind of kiss you savored because it brought you total bliss and led to panty melting ecstasy. With her hands at *his* waist, she couldn't help but explore the hills and valleys of his insanely chiseled physique. His body should be illegal, it was that good, and she wanted a front row seat to more of him. He was right, this kissing was really effing good.

He slowly pulled away, giving her a seductive half grin and knowing wink. He walked away, leaving her standing there doe-eyed and shocked, touching the lips he had just pleasured. He gave himself an imaginary high-five and double pat on the back.

Mission accomplished.

"Yes."

He tossed his gorgeous head back and let out the sexiest, throaty laugh she had ever heard.

FREE SAMPLE - RESCUED
CHAPTER 4

Sam drove home in a daze. It was a quick ten-minute drive anywhere in a town that size, but today she couldn't tell you if it was ten minutes, where she lived, or even what her name was. Dawson's soft full lips harassed her thoughts the entire drive, causing lust filled ideas that excited her and made her anxious, provoking every emotion in between.

Sam lived right outside of town, on the east side, the hospital stood on the west side. Being a tourist destination, summer months proved to be a bit more of a commute for such a small town. Rustic and charming, Main Street was just over a mile long, peppered with boutiques, coffee shops, restaurants, florists, and a variety of other shops on both sides of the lengthy stretch of road, and it was the epicenter of tourist season. During high season, which was most of the year, Main Street could get pretty congested with foot traffic and tourists venturing through.

The rodeo was in town, which provided even more delays. Their little town was busy! Sam took a country back road that ran along the south side of town, to avoid the delays. It was desolate, sprinkled with a few ranches and cabins, and held an incredible view of the mountains off in the distance. It was a nice drive, peaceful, and always reminded her why she loved living in McKenzie Ridge. She enjoyed the drive, and it was short, but it allowed her some quiet time to get lost in her thoughts.

Replaying the day's events, she was stunned by his kiss but more so by her reaction to it and desire for more of what he had to *offer*. He was purely intoxicating, like a drug, she decided, something one could become vastly addicted to and that she needed a lot more of. She could still smell him, feel him, *taste* him. This was a dangerous venture, sure to be loaded with equal parts pleasure and disappointment, but for the first time in years, she didn't care.

It was simply too easy to get lost in Dawson Tayler, and she didn't know why. He was simply another man, or was he? She had been a very successful hard ass, where men were concerned, for the last four plus years. Why was her libido coming out of hibernation now, and full throttle, for a man that was more dangerous than matches and gasoline? This was purely physical. She just needed to satisfy that long overdue craving, and this desire for Dawson would fade. Right?

She originally had pegged him as the love them and leave them type. Dawson was never in the company of another woman, ever, but a man like him doesn't sleep in a cold bed. She was sure his bed was plenty warm anytime he needed his itches scratched, and had plenty of women lining up, willing to scratch it, as often as needed. Sam was tempted to let him love her a couple rounds, warm those sheets for him, then leave him. Two birds, one man — take care of her own itch and get out before it got too serious and he left her. Her heart was safe that way.

There wasn't room in her life for a man, but maybe some lovin', some hot sweaty, grip the sheets and scream lovin'. That's all she could offer a man. He couldn't leave what he didn't have, and her heart would stay intact. She knew there was a genuine side to Dawson, a caring, considerate type, a great friend. She valued that newly found friendship, too, and didn't want to lose that. Maybe this was more than a hormone-enraged bout of temporary psychosis. Maybe there was more to this man than her previous assumptions. She was completely at war with herself and what she wanted from this man. Was she really considering this on any level?

She pulled into her driveway, unsure how she managed to get there in one piece, lost in her arousing thoughts of Dawson the entire way. When she walked in, she paused as a shiver drifted over her, raising the hairs ever so slightly on the back of her neck. The door was unlocked. She lived in a small, safe, uneventful town, but even so, she was always cautious and locked up, even if she was home.

Had she been so distracted and excited for her non-date lunch with Dawson that she didn't lock her door? She also left the lights on? Hairs still on end and instinct scratching, suggesting something was askew, she ultimately settled with the idea that she really needed to get her crap together and under control. Paranoid and forgetful were not characteristics she carried. She was becoming a distracted, sex-crazed loon over a man, and that just wasn't Sam.

This was the third time in so many weeks she had come home to find that she had left something out of order. First it was the sink running. Who does that? Then she came home to find the TV had been left on in her room and in the living room, and she didn't even remember having either on! Now the lights were on and the door unlocked? She found it as funny as she found it odd. She was acting like a love struck teenager, annoying as all get out.

Maybe after her *date*, she would find her senses again, remember why she didn't date, and pull it together. One night, it was all she needed to purge her system of Dawson's all-consuming, smexy presence in her world. There was a big difference between a *date* and *dating*. *Dating* required commitments that were easily broken and eventually led to disappointment, and a *date* is exactly what she needed to *cleanse her pallet* and satisfy a certain *ache.*

She walked next door to see Granny Lou and Everly for their weekly round table. Although they tended to get together more often than that as their lives overlapped in so many ways, especially being neighbors, they still carved out time to sit and enjoy each other uninterrupted, to catch up. These were the days they each looked forward to, getting together to devour Granny's famous snicker doodles or brownies a couple days a week. Girl time was important.

Evie still lived with her grandmother in the small guesthouse that rested behind the main house in the far corner of the property.

One day she would find a place of her own, but for now this was still home as it always had been. Her personal dwellings were quite small and simple as the main house was modest in size. It was only the two of them. She had her privacy, so she wasn't in a hurry to move on, and Lou loved having her granddaughter in close proximity.

Sam had her own small home, finally, after years in Granny Lou's house. Sam loved that woman. It was hard to leave, even if she was just next door. Granny was home to her. Her own mother couldn't be bothered to be anything but a reminder that Sam didn't hit the gene pool lottery.

When Sam's mother, *mother* used loosely, found a home for her daughter with Lou Shaw, she was quick to drop and run. Bette wasn't one to plant roots anywhere, which meant Sam didn't either, so finding McKenzie Ridge and a home where she could ditch her daughter made chasing her next husband become much easier, and Sam finally had stability in her life.

Lou couldn't stand the sight of Bette Morrison, didn't trust that woman any more than a rabid raccoon in the middle of the afternoon, but Lou was a fair woman, believed in second chances, or in this case twenty or thirty — people could change. Lou loved Sam, so she was happy to take her in and raise her as her own, especially when Bette needed to 'take a trip' that she would never come back from.

* * *

Evie was already in the sunroom sipping her coffee and eating cookies, eyeing Sam with a devilish grin as she came into the room. Sam halted in the doorway, completely aware of what was coming next. Small-town news travels fast. Rolling her eyes, Sam threw her head back, cheeks blushed, and quickly turned to retreat and avoid entering Evie's web of questions. She was here to eat sweets, not get grilled.

Fun, energetic, and kind spirited, Everly Shaw — jaws drop and heads turn when she's around. Her beautiful blonde hair, golden skin, and hazel eyes are like a ray of sunshine, pouring in. Tall, lean, toned in all the right places, she was hot, but she was choosing to live vicariously through Sam rather than find love herself.

Evie's parents died when she was nine. They were

killed in an accident while hiking. Evie was spared but spent two days alone with her deceased parents in the woods, waiting for rescue. Something like that changes a person. As a child it either enlivens you or completely screws you up. Evie had traces of both. Her childhood rooted her desire to be a nurse, but with adventure. Stationed at the same hospital as Sam, in the town where they were raised, Evie's days were filled with the excitement of helicopters, with her Life Flight assignments, and rappelling down cliffs to save lives as Search and Rescue. She was a real thrill seeker.

The appeal was adventure, but Sam and Granny Lou knew it was a distraction. Evie never talked about what happened to her family. Her family was Granny Lou, Sam, and the smallest lady of the house, little Ellie — they were her everything. That little girl changed all of their lives and softened the hardness that was Evie's heart — but only as much as a 4-year-old could. The most unlikely pair, opposites in every way, Evie and Sam were true soul sisters. She and Gran helped Sam through the early days of that whirlwind known as Ellie Lou — named after her and Gran in fact. Evie would do anything for the ladies in her life. Today, however, it was more about grilling Sam and enjoying every uncomfortable moment of embarrassment. This was going to be good.

"Hold up sister. Where do you think you're going? Seems you have some steamy news to tell, my friend!" Everly said while rubbing her hands together like a sinister old maid — the sinister part was solidified by the deep throaty chuckle that accompanied the wiggling eyebrows.

"Evie, please, you look like a starved piranha, and it's not a cute look on you," Sam replied in hopes of shaking the nagging dog off her scent. "I just want to stuff my face with some of those little bites of heaven over there or hide under a rock to avoid the nosey hen, lovingly known as you."

"Oh honey, you sit right here and stuff your face all you want while you explain that glow you've been carrying around. Something tells me it's called Dawson Tayler?" Everly said in a sassy southern drawl while fanning herself and batting her lashes.

"It's called tired and sweat. Its hot outside," Sam said in reference to this imaginary glow Everly was claiming. "And that *something* is called gossip. I swear this town is entirely too bored if my *non*-love life is the topic of town discussions."

Scooting her chair closer, Evie leaned in, elbows on the table, fully engrossed in Sam, letting it be known she was not leaving without the steamy details. "I would be sweating too if I was kissed so hard my lips swelled up like I just kissed the tail end of a wasp. This is going to be better than I thought…dish!"

"Ugh. Fine. We went to lunch at the Pavilion, which you obviously already know. I had a hoagie…"

"Eh! Nobody cares what you ate. Get to the good stuff where you two were kanoodling in the parking lot, sucking face, and rubbing each other's…"

"We weren't *kanoodling* or rubbing anything! I swear, Ev, this is so ridiculous. Look, we are just friends and…"

Granny Lou walked in with a fresh pot of coffee and a clever, well-informed look, before Sam could finish… knowing that look couldn't mean anything good. Not one to mince words, she bluntly questioned Sam, filling in the blanks that she apparently couldn't fill from the gossip mill.

"Have you decided what you are wearin' tomorrow night, and how was that kiss, honey?" Boom, there it was, shock and awe, Granny style. Sam considered making a run for it. "I hear it was a bit of a crowd pleaser, even if it was a little R rated. Thank goodness you had the good sense to keep your hands where they could be seen. It was the park after all, full of children, and Pastor Henry's wife, along with the Ladies of His Kingdom for their weekly meetin'."

Jaw dropped, eyes wide, and pink cheeks, Sam was completely mortified — beyond mortified, she was humiliated and felt the size of a gnat, the runt gnat in a family of freakishly small gnats. Sam left the park no more than 30 minutes ago, and that's being generous with time, so how on earth did Gran not only know the details of her afternoon 'kanoodling' in the park, but obviously already shared said details with her partner in crime, Everly, who was in full blown, head back, stomach holding, tears running, hysterics?

This was an all-time record for the McKenzie Ridge gossip brigade! Pastor Henry's wife and the Ladies of His Kingdom…she may as well add the scarlet letter to her attire, now, and paint her door red. These women, and likely a handful of men, deserved a damn medal — they officially broke the record for the ten mile radius grapevine event!

"So is everyone watching me or just your clan of vultures?" Sam shot back.

"Oh honey, don't be so dramatic. Carol called me from the park to tell me about her new granddaughter. You knew Sarah and Jack had the baby." Granny had a way of pleading innocence in a convincing way, over pretty much anything and everything. "Anyway, wouldn't you know it, she was at the park minding to the older ones, to give their mama some time to rest with the baby, and…"

"…and just happened to see me and Dawson and felt the need to spy for you?" Sam cutting Gran off would typically not happen, not due to respect or anything, but because

Louise Shaw rarely shared the floor when there was a story to tell, which is exactly why Sam cut in.

"Oh, Sam, you make it sound so calculated. 'Twas nothing more than a coincidence, honey," Granny said while shooing a hand at her because, of course, Sam's reaction was more ridiculous than the gossip mill, apparently.

Everly jumped in, tired of waiting for the good stuff, wishing she had popcorn for this one. She was rather enjoying the site of Sam squirming, a sign that this really was something and not the 'nothing' Sam claimed. "Yeah, Sam, it was a *coincidence*, so spill it. I'm currently living vicariously through you. My love life is null and void, so you and a couple of racy books are all I have to feel scandaliiized!"

"Ev, I don't have a *love* life! I don't date, you know that. I don't have time or the desire for it, and men are just…they are just more trouble than they are worth. The only thing scandalous about this is the flock of hens turning nothing into something," Sam defended.

"Well, if hot and heavy neckin' in a parkin' lot at the park is not datin' and a non-love life, things have changed since I was of age, girls," rebutted Gran, and she was about to drop the final bomb that should get Sam singing like a canary, Granny style. "Sounds like it was pretty steamy, left you speechless, and all."

"Wait, how did you know there was a date and the whole speechless thing?" Sam was flustered — damn this small town and its nosey geriatric mafia. "Where exactly was Carol watching me from, Gran?"

"Well honey, you parked right next to her! She was in the car, fixin' to leave when the two of you walked up. She felt it rude to interrupt by starting up her car." As if she should be flabbergasted by the idea of minding one's business by starting their car to leave. Granny may as well have just said 'duh.'

"Right, rude, more so than sitting in a car listening in. Let me guess, you were on the phone the whole time?"

"Well honey, I just told you that she had called to…"

"Right, right, tell you about the new baby. Got it." Sam planted her face firmly in her hands before resting it on the table. "How embarrassing!"

"This is hilarious, Sam! I bet half the old ladies in this town are getting steamy windows talking about it! This is awesome, epically awesome, Sam!" Everly could hardly catch her breath, laughing at her sister-friend and all her embarrassing shame. Not that she had anything to be ashamed of, but she was happy to let her think so. The show was just getting good. "Way to give the geriatrics something to look forward to!"

"Hey now, those old ladies are my friends, missy, and they are only looking out for our Sam. That Dawson is a dreamboat, hubba, hubba! He's the one they hope gets called in if one of their pacemakers should fail and they need a little mouth to mouth." Another slam dunk from Granny, earning her more eye rolling and pink cheeks from Sam, and cookie crumbs shooting through Everly's teeth as she laughed out loud.

"Oh geez, thanks for the visual, Gran. Sam, you need to warn your dream boat — sounds like there is a conspiracy over at the senior center to trap the guy into some covert, undercover naughty! Poor guy will be on a 'date' and not even know it!"

"I'm glad you find this so funny, Everly. Look, I appreciate the concern or support, whatever it is, but this is merely a friendly, friends, friend thing. Nothing more, nothing less.

We grab breakfast here and there, share some interests, it's like the male version of you, Evie!"

"Last I checked, you and I never swapped spit or did heavy petting body checks on each other in public places!"

"EVERLY! Okay, I am done talking about this. I can't even look at you right now, after that, eww. We are only having dinner, as FRIENDS, no big deal."

"Okay honey, friends it is." Granny chimed in. "Now finish that plate of snicker doodles before they find my ass. At my age, you don't even have to eat them for that to happen, and I need to keep this thing in shape so I can find my own neckin' partner."

"Gran!" Sam and Everly said in unison, completely shocked by Gran's need for lovin'.

"What?! I ain't dead yet! I may be old, but I'm still a lady that needs…"

"Whoa! Got it Gran!" Everly cut her off before it went from awkward to needing therapy.

"I'll stick to tea. I don't need the sugar or coffee keeping me up tonight. I went and left the door unlocked today. I don't get it. I could have sworn I locked it. I've left the lights, TVs, and even the water on lately, too."

"You don't think someone is over there meddlin', do ya?" Gran asked, ready to grab her gun and sleep over.

"No, Gran, nothing that dramatic ever happens in McKenzie Ridge. I just have a lot on my mind."

"You don't suppose that mama of yours has blowin' back through do ya? Somethin' she might do if she's in between husbands." Lou didn't trust Bette Morrison any more than she'd trust a hungry rabbit in her garden. Bette was as reliable as a bucket with a hole in it. She let Sam down more times than Granny cared to count.

"No, I haven't heard from her in a while. She was blissfully happy with what's his name last we spoke. Sneaky isn't her style. Her presence floods in long before her arrival, like a hurricane!"

There was a long pause before anyone spoke. Grinning ear to ear with a whimsy, daydream look in her eyes, Sam finally declared, "I will admit Dawson does have me a bit distracted. We may only be friends, but I am *not* blind."

Evie and Granny looked at each other grinning. Granny winked, "Friends my ass, honey."

FREE SAMPLE - RESCUED
CHAPTER 5

Dawson was nervous, and he was never nervous — especially when it came to women. No, he seeped self-assurance, both bold and brash, the epitome of confident. So why he felt this unfamiliar twinge of anxiety and nerves was beyond him. He was getting exactly what he wanted, a date with Sam, so why the sweat? Dawson was screwed. She had him completely by the balls, and he knew it — she probably did too.

Anxious emotions aside, he was open to this new territory as long as he got to explore it with Sam. She was intriguing and always on his mind. He found himself wondering what she would think or do in the various situations he found himself in. Ordering a milkshake, he wondered what kind Sam would like. Going for a run, Dawson wondered if Sam liked to run. Paint the walls Ecru or Toasted Wheat, wood or tile floors — what would Sam do? Although their pasts were different, he sensed a likeness between them, an interesting parallel that had him hooked.

He planned an evening at the rodeo since it was in town, followed by drinks and maybe a little dancing at The Pump House. The rest of the evening would be left to fate, but he hoped it lasted until morning. In his tight Wrangler jeans that hugged all the right places, putting his best assets on display, he had the hot cowboy look down. Black Stetson, white button-up, rolled sleeves, and boots — he was the inspiration for dirty dreams that made women cry *hee-haw*. Dawson was the kind of man who made a woman swoon simply by walking by. In those jeans, he made them cross their legs extra tight to avoid an embarrassing outburst. He was delicious.

Dawson stopped at Blooming Grounds to grab a bunch of flowers. He wasn't sure if flowers were the key to Sam's heart, but he hadn't met a woman who hated flowers, so he had nothing to lose. Roses were sexy, like Sam, but they were also a lot of other things neither of them were ready for. Thoughtful and kind, gentlemanly, that was what he was going for tonight. Roses would come later — dozens upon dozens of roses — should things go as he wanted them to. Dawson searched through the array of flowers when he landed on the perfect bouquet: daisies. They were simple, cute, understated, and perfectly Sam.

Sam answered the door looking like every cowboy's wet dream, her slate blue eyes captivating and long dark tresses falling in soft curls around her shoulders. She wore a red button-up blouse, sans sleeves, that tied at the waist, showing just enough of her flat, tan stomach to keep his eyes traveling south. His pants were getting tighter as he gazed over her perfectly fitted jean skirt that hugged her ass and left her perfectly shaped thighs exposed. Even the well-worn cowboy boots were making him hot and painfully bothered.

He handed her the daisies, and stuttered, "Th-These are for me. From me! I mean, these are for you."

Man alive, she had him between a rock and hard place — literally — and that outfit had him already picturing it lying around her sexy boots. He was a goner, and clearly, he could no longer speak coherently. He found her stunning, even in her scrubs, but tonight, she took his breath away. She was a sexy little piece of heaven standing before him. Thank you, Jesus.

Sam drank in the tall, dark, and handsome cowboy in front of her. He looked so good, it was almost cliché. She felt her face heat, her palms sweat, and her womanhood awaken at the sound of the alarm her most private parts were sounding. She was screwed, or would be shortly, if the night ended the way she had been daydreaming about the past twenty-four hours, thanks to that kiss. Dawson Tayler had her in the palm of his hand, and she hoped he knew it as much as she hoped he didn't. He was as much dangerous in that outfit as he was sexy, and she had no idea how she would make it through the night with her clothes still on.

She decided in that moment the question she had been pondering for some time now was obvious. She wasn't looking for love, but a romp in the sack with this bucking bull, and it was going to happen. The cowboy look granted her clarity and delivered the answers to everything she had been questioning about Dawson Tayler. She needed to get sweaty with this man, get him out of her system in a down and dirty, naked kind of sweat, and she wasn't ashamed at all.

"Daisies are my favorite. That was very sweaty. Sweet! Man, it's hot today — uh…thank you."

Granny Lou walked up to say hello to Dawson, and, of course, check out his ass in those jeans so she would have something to report back to the geriatric mafia — and because she wasn't dead yet, as she would say. She commented on the lovely flowers, offering to take them in and put them in water so they could get on their way. She promised to lock up after she grabbed a certain bag she had been there to pick up in the first place.

"Now, you two have a good time tonight. I won't expect to see ya 'til morning. Ride 'em cowboy, yee-haw!" She gave them a wink, and Sam a quick elbow bump to the ribs, giggling all the way inside. "Friends my ass."

* * *

Ending just short of the curve of her ass, he couldn't help but notice the rise of her skirt, which led to his own rise as he helped her into his truck. Thank God for tall trucks and short skirts. Dawson wished he had a taller truck. This was going to be the longest, stiffest, ten-minute drive of his life. She was going to be his undoing. Lord, have mercy, he couldn't wait.

Sam was delightfully aware of the effect she was having on Dawson by the sweat gathering at his brow, the fact that he wouldn't even look her way the entire drive, and because he kept clearing his throat, but didn't say a word. She was also painfully aware of what a turn on it was knowing what she was doing to him. Tonight would be full of sitting sideways and crossed legs. Oh yes, turned-on cowboy Dawson was much hotter than everyday hot Dawson. Sweet Jesus, this was the best idea she'd had in a very long time. She would pray for her sins later.

The quick drive allowed him to gather his thoughts and get his raging hormones under control. In a matter of minutes, a short skirt clad ass managed to set him back a couple decades, to teenage boy hell, where the word *boob* was enough to embarrass him in a not so becoming way. What was it with this woman? How did she manage to get under his skin after all this time? What was different about tonight, and why hadn't he thought of this sooner?

* * *

Regaining his composure, he held her hand, helping her out of the truck and never letting it go. He was pushing her boundaries, and she was beginning to like it — a lot. Sam managed to throw out her independent, *I don't need a man* tendencies without a single inner feminist protest. She enjoyed Dawson leading the way, taking charge, taking care of her. She felt nurtured and cared for, and it was a fucking turn on. His alpha swagger was sexy and hot, and she'd follow it anywhere. The eyes of every single woman they passed, and some not so single women, tracked him everywhere they went, followed by deep, throaty "ohs" and breathy sighs. She didn't blame them at all. He was smoldering with those emerald eyes, unshaven face, and panty-melting body perfectly traced in his well-fitted ensemble. The only thing that came to mind, aside from the fact he was *hers,* was *hands off, bitches.*

They ate barbeque — anything else at a rodeo would be sacrilege — and drank local brews in between events. They watched tie-down roping and bull riding, which oddly took both of their minds to dirty places full of rope tying and *riding* of the naked, sexy kind. Thank God for the kids' barrel racing on stick ponies and the children's finale mutton bustin' to chill the inappropriate ideas like a cold ass shower. He held her close all evening, either with his arm around her or hand in hand, making a statement to anyone wondering — he was with *his* girl. It was a glorious night.

***

The main events were over for the night, and the rowdy rodeo party scene was commencing, so they went to The Pump House for a drink before calling it a night. An old-time gas station, converted to roadhouse style bar, with booze, pool, dancing, and the best food in town, it was a safe place. There was little to do in such a small town, but neither wanted the night to end quite yet. In fact, it was really just beginning.

It wasn't lost on Sam that Dawson was a gentleman at every turn, and not in a superficial attempt at anything. He was genuine, kind, and real. His mannerisms were instinctive. As alpha as he was, he was equally as gentle. He held the door for her, pulled out her chair, even went for their drinks, and served her. Dawson was charming the pants off her, and she knew it was for no reason other than being who he was.

The conversation was light in the beginning, as it had been most of the day, mostly about the rodeo, the beautiful weather, and even work. He couldn't take his eyes off hers or keep his hands to himself. If Dawson wasn't holding her hand, he had his hand at the small of her back. By the end of the night, he had his arm over her shoulder, and she leaned into him, a perfect fit, as if he was built for her and vice versa.

He could feel those walls of hers crumbling, little by little, and he was pleased by that. The message they were sending to everyone they ran into was that they were, indeed, *dating*, and Sam seemed totally at ease with that unspoken statement. Dawson liked what that implied, because in a matter of days, his decade long rules had all been broken, and he wasn't planning to reinstate a single one.

She was absolutely entranced by this man. His actions went beyond just charm. He was caring, doting even, but in a non-suffocating way. Dawson was a god to look at, a man's man with his confident swagger, and completely gentle while seductive with his touch. She drank him in and couldn't seem to get enough. He knew how to treat a woman, and she couldn't wait to see how he handled one in bed or wherever they ended up next. Every time she had those kinky thoughts, her body hummed and heated all over. She was beginning to crave him.

The Pump House was packed. Everyone they knew was there, but they still managed to find a semi private two-top booth in the corner. Dawson grabbed a couple beers while she grabbed the table and watched him work his way through the room. He was such a force, he commanded the room in a way that demanded respect, appreciation, and no one minded paying it, it seemed. It was turning into the kind of night she could get used to. This *one night, get him out of my system* idea might actually become several nights. He was her new drug, one she was already addicted to, and she hadn't even felt the high yet.

This was the first time they went together alone. The Pump House was safe for them both. Out in the open, very public, and not too intimate…thank God. They knew everyone there, which was a nice distraction from the thoughts crossing both their minds. Keep it clean — that was Dawson's mantra all night. Anytime his gaze drifted below her chin, a hoot or holler from the pool tables would pull his mind from the gutter, reminding him they weren't alone. Sam was mesmerizing. He found himself wanting to know more, not just *see* more.

No raw emotions, simply friendship and whatever seductive, carnal benefits that came with it. She could handle that.

She needed that badly. Dawson had her wound up so tight, she was going to erupt in a most embarrassing way, simply by watching the man. She was letting her guard down, slowly, letting him in, and as much as she appreciated him beyond the physical, she had to keep her wits about her and not let her heart get involved. But that was becoming quite the task as her heart was leading the way.

He returned with two beers, a couple glasses of water, and a basket of peanuts. He had thought of everything. They got part way through their mugs and some safe insignificant chatter when the music got louder and the crowd got larger. They took to the floor, where very little was spoken, but a lot was said.

The Pump House catered to every genre of music. Tonight was upbeat and energetic, crossing the decades with their song and dance. The crowd cheered as the theme seemed to lean more toward country, likely due to the rodeo and all its cowboys in town. They enjoyed themselves. It was fun and comfortable and maybe a little sexy, each impressed by what the other brought to the evening and left on the dancefloor. They gave it their all and worked it to a few line dances, a two-step, and even a swing.

They had danced a hundred times at The Pump House, but tonight, they each saw the other in a different light, each wanting to impress the other, and both succeeding. There was something unintentionally seductive about their dancing. They couldn't keep their eyes or hands off each other.

Hot, sweating, and exhausted, Dawson was headed to the table when he noticed she had stayed on the dancefloor. She was looking right at him, intentions made clear with just a look. Her eyes were heavy, cheeks flushed, and she started dancing…for him.

It was one of those sexy, tantalizing, shake-your-ass,

have-no-shame dances, and she embraced every opportunity to swing and display her offer. She was in the line, doing the dance, watching him over her shoulder, captivating him as she shook exactly what he wanted. She had an extra sway in her hips, move to her ass, and ground it around, bending over a bit more than necessary, seducing him with every alluring move.

She ran her hands through her hair, tossing her head back in a provocative manner, licking her lips as she turned back to him, knowing exactly what she was doing. His pants were so tight, it hurt. She had him in the palm of her dainty little hand. She wanted him. She was his muse. She was his.

The song ended, and she started off to their table when he wrapped his arm around her waist and held her close, keeping her where she was. It was a slow song — neither could tell what, nor did they care, and they danced. He asked her if that intoxicating number was for him, and she nodded with a devilish grin. Dawson held her closer so she could feel his arousal, so she could see what she did to him, and then he kissed her — hard, purposeful, and full of invitation and wicked intention.

She accepted it and gave back as much as she received. She kissed him with everything she had, rubbing her body against him like a secret lap dance only he could see and feel. Not sure how he broke down her walls, she got lost in him, not caring where they were or who was watching the thrill Dawson was giving her. She couldn't taste enough of him. His leg between hers, chest to chest, they ground and danced a little dirty. The message to everyone around was clear: territory was undeniably marked, they were certainly a couple.

The song ended, and they just stood there, locked in each other's gaze, body to body, heated and primed, when Dawson broke the drawn-out silence. "Do you want to get out of here? Get some...air?"

She smiled. "I haven't finished my beer."

With a sly grin and a wink, Dawson said, "I'll buy you a six pack, darlin'. Let's go!"

She laughed out loud as he pulled her through the crowd. He opened her door, and took another long, wet kiss with her back against his truck. Hands slid down her sides and landed on her firm ass that fit in his hands perfectly. She ran her hands through his hair and let out a slight mewl as he squeezed. Hands rising to her waist, Dawson lifted her into the truck before breaking the kiss.

Bear Creek ran along the outskirts of town, crossing through Pavilion Park to the woods on the other side. More than a sprinkle of a creek, not quite a river, it hosted a plethora of wildlife and many banks to fish and catch crawdads. Dawson drove to a spot where he liked to drop in a line and ponder his thoughts from time to time. It was peaceful, grounding. Tonight, it boasted privacy, surrounded by trees and untouched wilderness — a moonlit rendezvous to ponder something new.

Sam was taken by the beauty the light of the moon cast across the creek, like nature's mirror, displaying its allure in a perfect reflection, surrounded by the millions of stars twinkling like precious gems above them. The magnificence of their surroundings was breathtaking by day, and by night, it was absolutely enchanting, intensifying their already heightened mood and senses. Here, it was just them and the simplest sounds of nature.

It was a warm summer night, but he was hot from the

company. Dawson grabbed a blanket from the back seat of his truck and placed it at the bank's edge where he led her.

"Wow, you come prepared, Tayler," she teased.

"I'm a medic. I have a hefty first aid kit, matches, kindling, and even food rations if you're hungry. I'm prepared for anything. We could survive for days out here if you wanted," he rebutted, half joking, half serious. Dawson wouldn't mind being stranded somewhere secluded with the woman before him. He could get lost in her for days.

"Is that some sort of offer, cowboy?" she tempted, hoping it was indeed some sort of offer. Getting lost with Dawson sounded like a naughty dream come true.

"Do you want it to be?" he questioned her, surprised at the breath he was holding, hoping for a yes.

"I want it to be something," Sam admitted, shocked she said it so freely, but she did indeed want more from Dawson. Friendzone with Dawson was great, but for the first time in years, she desired more. Dawson was proving to be the exception to every rule she had.

"How about we start with this." He grabbed her hand and walked her to the center of the blanket, right at the water's edge, and kissed her, long and with promise.

He felt her soften in his arms, and she kissed him back. It was full of passion, vulnerability, and surrender. Dawson felt her walls falling as she invited him in, boundaries no longer distancing them, allowing what they both hadn't known they wanted all along. He had been waiting on this moment all night, the chance to get lost in her, and by her reaction, it seemed certain she had been wanting that too.

Sam let go of his hands and dragged hers up his torso, placing them on his hard chest. Her hands traveled up his body, exploring every bump and ridge. The man was fucking ripped. As her hands found their way around his neck, his trailed up and down her sides, full of equal parts care and mischief. Each time they rose, they came closer to her breasts, teasing her. Her body was humming from the sensation and anticipation of what was to come. She arched into him, rubbing her chest to his, sending a seductive message, inviting more of his touch.

He was desperate to feel more, stroke more, and even *taste* more. If he wasn't careful, this was going to end before it even got started. She had him wound so tight, on the edge of delirium. He pictured her wicked little dance, the sway of her hips, the shake of her ass, the bow of her back, and the curve of her breasts. He was in deep, and completely content at the realization. She had cast her spell on him, and Dawson hoped it never broke.

His hands didn't stop this time as he cupped her breasts. Full and firm, they fit his grip perfectly, exquisitely made only for him. The feel of her in his hands was paralyzing. He wanted to see her, all of her, in every way. As he gently squeezed, she moaned a deep, sensual sound that unraveled him. He began to unbutton her shirt, exposing her beautiful sun-kissed skin, taking his breath away with her beauty and allure. He was in trouble.

Sam broke the kiss, winded and overwhelmed by sensation. She stared into his eyes, seeing his desire flowing, as easy to read as the thoughtful care he was taking with her. Dawson looked at her, searching for permission to continue, when she reached for him, hands roaming under his shirt, feeling him, skin to skin. She wanted more, *needed* more of what he was giving her.

She wore black and red lace, a clear indication she dressed for this very moment. He trailed her skin, from her mouth to her neck, slowly and seductively making his way to heaven. Sam threw her head back from the intense pleasure as

Dawson reached her breasts and began an assault so erotic, she could hardly stand it.

He bit at her pebbled nipples through the delicate lace and slid one strap down her soft shoulder. As he made his way to her other breast, claiming it as he had the last, he freed the remaining strap. Dawson stood back, looked her in the eyes, and waited for her, letting her decide just how far they did or didn't go.

She gazed up at him through the thick lashes of her hooded eyes. She was hungry for more, wanted more, desperate to be satiated. Entranced by all that was Dawson, she boldly reached up and released the clasp, removing the thin barrier between them. She watched the black and red lace fall to her feet, then tilted her head as she met his eyes while she unbuttoned his shirt and dropped it from his shoulders. The man was a God, more than she had imagined, and she'd imagined it often.

She licked her lips in a provocative way as she traced her hands down his hard chest, straight to his belt buckle. She did her work to open his belt, then his pants. He was completely hard for her, and it turned her on, pleasured her to know *she* did that to him. Still confined, she slid her hand over his manhood, making him moan as he stood there in nothing but his tight boxer briefs that left near nothing to the imagination. God was an artist.

Dawson drank her in, so beautiful, so perfect, a sexy little vixen, so ready for him. At her touch, he took her mouth again, took her breasts in his hands, and began to tweak her rosy hardened buds with his fingers. The action was so carnal, her body heated, and her legs went weak. He lowered her to the ground, their feet resting in the water, never losing contact as he began his descent, down her neck, to her collarbone, where he licked and nipped, and finally to his destination where he took her hard nipple into his mouth and went to work.

She moaned as Dawson held one nipple in his mouth and the other between his fingers. Never had she felt such satisfaction, and they were only at foreplay. She wanted more from him — and of him. She slid her hand down his abs until she found his girth, then stilled for a moment at his size. Dawson really was a god. Gently, she stroked him, causing deep, throaty moans from them both. He carefully wrapped his hand around hers, moving it to his side, and began to remove her skirt.

He felt her quiver beneath him, anxious, or excited, or both, as his hand made its way down her body, resting on her mound. He found her matching black and red panties damp, and smiled while holding her nipple between his teeth. She was so ready for him, but he wasn't done yet.

He slipped a finger into the side of her sexy panties and began to glide over her slick folds. Dawson caressed her, making her jerk in eager movements before his mouth drifted from her breasts and headed south. Her breasts were perfect, and he found them hot as hell. He would find his way back to them before the night was over — that was a promise.

He stroked her sex once more before slipping his finger inside her. She was so hot, wet, and tight. He worked her over, slipping in a second finger, preparing her for what was to come. As his mouth trailed her abdomen with certain intent, he rested a kiss on each hip before landing right on her heat. Dawson tasted her. She was heaven, sweet, warm, and spicy — completely Sam.

She cried out as he took her into his mouth, tilting her hips, adjusting for him, inviting him. His mouth, his tongue, his fingers, it was almost too much as her body hummed and she cried out his name. She lifted her hips and tilted into his mouth, greedy for his pleasure. He read her like a book, completely consumed by her need for more. He reached for her breast, rolling her nipple between his fingers while still stroking her with his tongue and fingers, and she unraveled beneath him with a scream. Dawson Tayler was her undoing.

As hard as he'd ever been, ready to come apart, he pulled her to his lap while she still soared through her ecstasy. Wrapping her legs around him, they sat waist deep in the warm summer's water, under the glowing spotlight of the moon. Dawson looked at her satisfied expression, and was totally lost in her, wanted her, needed her. He didn't want this night to ever end.

As if she knew what he was waiting for, she nodded her head, giving him permission to take her completely. He finally entered her with all his boldness, and covered her mouth with his, muffling her moans. He loved her slowly, deeply, and wholly, until he freed every last bit of himself while she soared again — this time, not alone.

They lay wrapped in the blanket, attempting to dry off and come down from the high they'd reached together. Sloshing her foot in the water, she found herself giggling like a schoolgirl. She was lying naked in the middle of a forest, late into the night, next to a really hot, really naked guy. He glanced at her with a mischievous grin, as if he knew what she was thinking.

She didn't know what had just come over her, perhaps those adorable dimples? Following her playful instincts, she lifted her foot, bringing a splash of water with it, soaking him. She quickly got up and started running up the shallow edge of the water. She didn't make it far before large hands whisked her up and he ran toward the center.

At its deepest point, he paused to quickly kiss her. His devilish wink and grin were the last thing she saw before he launched her into the water. Not to be outdone, she grabbed his ankles beneath the water, bringing him down with her. They played like this for some time, muscles aching from their laughter, before ending up in each other's arms again, giving nature a slow, intimate show.

Although hesitant, Dawson began to help her dress. He was gentle, caring, and considerate with kisses in between. He finally folded the blanket, their blanket, and held her close all the way up to the bank where the truck was parked. He loved on her some more before he helped her inside where they sat for a bit longer, not ready to leave this place now marked as theirs.

* * *

He drove her home in silence, holding her hand the whole way, both with lazy, satisfied smiles. He parked in her driveway, opened her door for her, and walked her to the front porch.

"Thank you," she whispered, her head against his chest, words full of meaning.

She wasn't thanking him for the epic outdoor sex on the edge of a creek, in the middle of a deserted forest, amongst the woodland creatures, although worthy of praise. She was thanking him for being careful with her heart. Wanting to say more, but leaving it at that, lost for words, she looked at him, drinking in his sweet smile, knowing he understood the meaning hidden within her sparse words.

"I had…" he paused, searching for the right words to define this night, words that said everything without saying too much, "…an amazing time. More than I thought I could have. I hope this is a first and not a last, because I'm not sure how I would feel about that." He hesitated, deciding less was more in this moment. He pulled her close and kissed her tenderly, and it felt like home.

"I'll see you at work tomorrow?" he asked, then gently kissed her forehead before she could answer and walked away. As he climbed in his truck and paused, propping himself between the open door and cab, he looked at her with an admiring smile and quick wink before driving off.

Sam fell against the closing door as she went inside, completely spent and with dreamy eyes, wondering how on earth they would ever top this night and all it represented. She really needed to reconsider this non-dating thing.

"Wow!"

CLICK HERE TO CONTINUE READING RESCUED

Made in the USA
Coppell, TX
23 June 2021

57922820R10125